THE COLLECTED TALES OF PIERRE LOUŸS

ILLUSTRATED BY
SIÉGEL

Fredonia Books
Amsterdam, The Netherlands

The Collected Tales of Pierre Louÿs

by
Pierre Louÿs

ISBN: 1-58963-989-8

Reprinted from the 1930 edition

Fredonia Books
Amsterdam, The Netherlands
http://www.fredoniabooks.com

TABLE *of* CONTENTS

THE COLLECTED TALES
OF PIERRE LOUŸS

PART I

LEDA

or The Blessing of Darkness

The night was profound. Artemis hunted unseen beneath the silver crescent that surmounted the black branches, and through them millions of stars peered at the listening earth. The four Corinthians lay upon the grass near the three young men; and it seemed as if no sound would ever again break upon the silent world.

Stories should be told only in the sunlight. When the shadows have closed in, the fabulous voices are heard no more, for the wandering spirit comes to rest and communes mysteriously with itself.

Each of the outstretched women already had a secret companion which she created charmingly in the image of her youthful fancy. But their eyes lifted in the darkness when grave Melandryon addressed them thus:

"The events I will relate to you concern the Swan and the little nymph who dwelt upon the banks of the river Eurotas. It reveals the blessing of darkness."

He half raised himself, and with one hand resting among the whispering grasses, began to speak:

I

In those far-off days, one did not find throughout the land the tombs of dead men or the temples of living gods. Few humans existed; none spoke. The earth was the playground of the gods and the scene of miraculous births. It was in those times that Echidna was delivered of the Chimera and Pasiphæ of the Minotaur. Little children paled at the thought of great dragons that haunted the woods.

Upon the misty borders of the river Eurotas, where the foliage was so thick that one never saw the sun, lived a wonderful young girl who was bluish like the night, cool as the white moon, and soft as the milky-way. For this reason, she was called Leda.

In her veins flowed the blood of the iris and not, as in yours, the blood of roses; so that her nails were bluer than her hands, her nipples bluer than her breasts, while her elbows and knees were pure cerulean. Her lips matched the tint of her eyes, which were blue as the deep water. Her hair flowed sombre and blue as the midnight sky and quickened so along her arms as to give it the appearance of wings.

She loved only water and the dark. Her delight was in walking along the spongy fields near the shores, where she could feel the water without seeing it, and her bare feet shivered with pleasure at the hidden moisture.

She never actually bathed herself in the river, for she feared the malice of the naiads; and, beside, she shrank from giving herself wholly to the water. But how she loved its cool wetness! She would dip the extreme curl of her hair in the swirling current and then draw it deliciously over her pale skin in slow fantastic designs. Other times she would make a little cup of her hands to hold the water and then let it run between her young breasts to lose itself in the curve of her rounded legs. Or else she would extend her slim length on the damp moss and drink softly from the flowing stream, like a silent hind.

This was her life; and in her mind, very often now, was the thought of the satyrs. She saw them sometimes at a distance, but they always fled from her in fright, taking her for Phœbe who dealt cruelly with those who came upon her naked. She wished that they would pause so that she might talk with

them. The details of their appearance filled her with amazement. One night, when she had retreated into the forest, because rain had flooded the banks of the river, she had seen closely one of these demi-gods as he slept; but, seized with fright in her turn, she had run away before he awakened. Afterward, she would come back to that place at intervals, drawn by some force she did not understand.

Then she began to contemplate her own person, and found that mysterious, too. At this period a strange longing took possession of her and often she wept in her hair.

When the moon shone clear, she regarded herself in the river's mirror. It struck her that it might look well to gather up her hair in order to show her neck which, she perceived, was very lovely beneath it. A supple rush sufficed to confine the thick blue knot, and over this she laid a coronet which she made of five large aquatic leaves and a spreading water lily.

At first she found a simple pleasure in walking about thus. But no one saw her, for she was always alone. Somehow she became unhappy about this, and lost interest in her games.

Although she knew it not, her body was even now listening for the flutter of the Swan's wings.

II

It was evening. Half awake, she was reflecting on resuming her dreams, as she vaguely contemplated a long stream of yellow day still shining beyond the night of the forest, when she was startled by a commotion in the nearby reeds. Then she saw a most beautiful Swan.

The resplendent bird was white as a woman, roseate as the day, and radiant as a cloud. He seemed the very spirit of the noon-day sky, its form, its winged essence. That is why he was known as Zeus.

Leda, astonished, watched the movements of his glorious outspread wings. He circled about her at a distance, gazing at her sideways. Then he drew closer and, raising himself on his wide, red feet, stretched the undulous grace of his neck as high as he could over the young bluish thighs, to the soft fold of the hip.

The nymph's tremulous hands lightly touched the little head, enveloping it with caresses. The bird quivered in all his feathers. He clasped and bent her naked legs. Leda let herself be borne to the ground.

Swiftly her two hands flew to cover her eyes. Yet she felt neither fear nor shame but an inexplicable joy; and her young breasts swelled with the beating of her heart.

She divined nothing of what was going to

happen. What could happen? She understood nothing, not even why her heart sang with joy, as she felt along her arms the supple neck of the Swan.

Why had he come? What had she done to draw him to her? Why had he not flown away like the other swans on the river or the satyrs of the forest? She had always lived alone, from her earliest memories. She had not therefore many ideas to ponder and none certainly that helped her now. . . This Swan . . . this Swan. . . She had not called him, she had not even seen him, for she had been asleep. Yet he had come.

She no longer felt afraid to open her eyes, but she did not stir for fear of making him fly away. She felt upon her burning cheeks the freshness of his beating wings.

Soon he seemed to recoil and his caresses changed. Leda opened herself to him like a blue flower of the river. Her cold knees thrilled to the warmth of the bird's body. Suddenly she cried:

"Ah! . . Ah! . ."

And her arms quivered like pale branches. His beak had penetrated her, terribly, and within her the head of the Swan moved violently, as though he were ardently ravishing her entrails.

A long shuddering sob of abundant felicity shook her body. With closed eyes, she let her burning head fall backward, and her trembling fingers tore at the grass; then her little convulsed feet finally spread themselves out in the silence.

For a long time she lay motionless. The first movement her hands made met the ensanguined beak of the Swan upon her bosom. The great white bird loomed against the clear sheen of the water. She tried to rise, but he obstructed her. She wished to take a little water in the hollow of her hand and cool her joyous pain; the bird stopped her with his great wing.

Passionately she encircled him in her arms and covered with kisses his tufted plumes which bristled up under her mouth. Then she sank back on the ground and slept heavily.

. . .

The next morning she was awakened at the break of day by a new sensation, and it seemed to her that something detached itself from her body. This was a large, blue egg which had rolled in front of her, gleaming like a sapphire.

Wondering, she wished to take it up and play with it, or perhaps bake it in hot embers as she had seen the satyrs do, but the Swan seized it in his beak and placed it under a cluster of bending reeds. Then he stretched his wings over it, regarding Leda steadily, and, in a straight flight toward the sky, slowly soared so high that he melted into the brightening dawn with the last pale star.

[12]

III

Leda looked for him at the next rising of the stars, awaiting him among the reeds of the river, near the blue egg which had been born of their miraculous union.

The Eurotas was peopled with swans, but the one she sought was no longer there. She would have known him among a thousand and, even with her eyes closed, she would have sensed his approach. But he was not there; of this she was quite certain.

She removed her wreath of water leaves, let it fall unheeded into the stream, shook down her night-blue hair and wept into it.

When she wiped her eyes at last and looked about, a satyr, whose steps she had not heard, stood gazing at her.

For she was no longer like Phœbe. She had lost her virginity. The satyrs were not afraid of her any more. She sprang to her feet and drew back in fright. The ægipan said to her, gently:

"Who art thou?"

"I am Leda," she answered.

He was silent for a moment, then he asked her:

"Why art thou not like the other nymphs? Why art thou blue like the water and the night?"

[13]

"I do not know."

He regarded her for some moments in astonishment. "What dost thou here," he asked, "—all alone?"

"I await the Swan." And she turned her eyes towards the river.

"What swan?"

"The Swan. I did not call him, I had never seen him, and he came. I am so astonished. I will tell thee." And she related to him all that had happened, parting the reeds to show him the blue egg of the morning.

The satyr understood. He began to laugh and give her coarse explanations. She stopped him at each word, putting her hand over his mouth; and she cried:

"No, no, I do not wish to know. I will not. Oh! thou hast told me! Is this possible! Now I can no longer love him and I shall be unhappy enough to die."

He seized her by her two arms, passionately.

"Do not touch me!" she moaned. "Oh! how happy I was this morning! I did not know how happy I was! Now, if he returns, I shall love him no longer. Now thou hast told me! Ah, how wicked thou art!"

He clasped her suddenly and caressed her hair.

"Oh! No! No! No! . . No!" she cried again and again, "Not thee! Oh! not that! Oh! The Swan! If he should return. . . Alas! Alas! All is ended, all is over."

She remained with open eyes, not weeping, her mouth open, her hands trembling with fright.

"I wish I could die. I know not even whether I am mortal. I wish I could die in the water, but I am afraid of the naiads and that they would carry me away with them. Oh! What have I done!"

And she sobbed loudly upon her arms. But a grave voice aroused her and, when she opened her eyes, she saw the god of the river, crowned with green grasses, who stood half out of the water, leaning upon an oar of bright wood.

He spoke to her:

"Thou art the night. And thou hast loved the symbol of all which is bright and glorious. Thou hast united thyself to it. From the symbol is born the symbol and from the symbol shall be born Beauty. It is in the blue egg which has come forth from thee. Since the beginning of the world, it was known that she would be called Helen; and he who shall be the last man shall know that she lived.

"Thou has been filled with love because thou hast known nothing. That is the blessing of darkness. But thou art also a woman and, on the evening of the same day, man also has impregnated thee. Thou bearest within thyself the shadowy being who knows nothing of itself; whom its father has not foreseen and whom its son would ignore. I shall take the germ in my waters. It shall remain in oblivion.

"Thou hast been full of hatred because thou hast learned all. And I will make thee forget all. This is the blessing of darkness."

She did not quite understand what he had said, but she thanked him, weeping. Then she entered into the bed of the river and cleansed herself there of the satyr. And when she returned to the bank, she had lost all remembrance of her grief and of her happiness.

. . . .

Melandryon ceased speaking. The women remained silent for a little space. Then Rhea asked:

"And Castor and Polydeuces? Thou hast said nothing concerning them. Yet they were Helen's brothers."

"No. That legend is false, for it was Helen alone who was born of the Swan."

"How knowest thou? And why sayest thou that the Swan wounded her with his beak? That is not in the legend and it is not probable. . . And why sayest thou that Leda was blue like the water and the night? Thou hast a reason!"

"Didst thou not hear the words of the River? Symbols should never be explained. They should never be penetrated. Have faith, do not doubt. That which figures as a symbol hides a truth, but it is not made manifest. For, otherwise, why should it be symbolized? Forms should not be rent, for they conceal only the Invisible. We know that there are adorable nymphs hidden in the trees and that, when the woodcutter opens them, the hamadryads are already dead. We know that, behind us, there are dancing satyrs and divine nudities; but we should not turn: all would have already vanished.

"The undulous reflection of the springs is the spirit of the naiad. The buck erect amidst the goats is the reality of the satyr. One or another among you is the essence of Aphrodite. But it is not to be spoken, it is not to be known, one should not try to fathom it. Such is the condition of love and of happiness.

"That is the blessing of darkness."

ARIADNE

or The Pathway of Peace

Now, having come to a cavern, the most awesome, the most profound of the whole forest, so abandoned by men and beasts that the very silence seemed to have been absorbed into something still more inexpressible, the Corinthians drew back. Their hands faltered to their temples, their eyes stared unseeingly, and their lips parted but no sound escaped.

Tremblingly, as they felt themselves impelled by the darkness, they shrank close to one another as the poor lost souls of the dead press together before the portal of Hades in a last effort to escape their doom.

The voice of Thrases drew them from their dazed inertia.

"Assuredly," he said, "this is one of the entrances to Tartarus; but there is no need to be affrighted; for none of you will glimpse the black torches of Persephone before the day fixed by the Keres. Moreover, that is a happy day which should be welcomed with joy. . ."

"I do not wish to die," said Rhea.

"O Thrases, what art thou saying?" inquired sage Amaryllis. "For death hath terrors for me also, and my soul cannot remain indifferent when I dream of it."

Thrases did not argue. He wished to avoid the weariness of too obvious reflections, and,

[21]

for his own pleasure, wreathed his thought intricately into an obscure and subtle tale.

The Corinthians had seated themselves on a long block of polished rock. He, meanwhile, remained standing near Clinias and Melandryon, the first too distracted to comprehend, the second too wise to listen.

He began with hesitation, as though reluctant to break the silence, and his voice was low and far away.

I

A forest of cedars.

Evening.

Seven young men and seven young girls advanced, hand in hand. They had come from Attica, upon a ship with black sails. And one of them was Theseus, son of Ægeus, son of Pandion, son of Cecrops, son of Erechtheus.

Green palms! coronals of oak leaves! cries! triumphs! laurels! outstretched hands! accompany the Heroes. . .

They had come from Attica, upon a ship with black sails. And all, during the funereal journey, had pledged themselves, two by two, to find each other again, beyond death, among the indolent fields of asphodel; beyond the horrible death for which they were destined by the human Bull, fruit of the shame of Pasiphæ. They had pledged themselves. Yet two among them remained apart: the hero Theseus, proud and confident, and the virgin Myris who walked beside him.

Under the horizontal foliage of the cedars, through the thin plantings of the forest, the long rays from the west ran out like sword blades, impalpable and transparent. The condemned ones, hand clasped in hand, slowly traversed these great weapons of the sun, knowing exactly how many intervened between them and the entrance of the Labyrinth. And after the last one would descend the fateful night.

So they thought, at least; but Theseus and Myris had other certainties.

They advanced, two by two. At last they arrived.

But they had not yet passed the last ray of the sun when they heard, behind them, a quick step on the dead leaves. They turned and saw a woman standing there.

She was of noble stature, well shod with tight leather straps and clad in the short tunic worn by the followers of Artemis: the white cloth, fastened at the shoulders with two clasps of beaten gold, confined at the girdle, and reaching just to the dainty knees. A silver diadem gleamed beneath the thick luxuriance of her hair, part of which was twisted in plaits and part tucked up in a Laconian knot with a certain heedless grace. Her brown eyes sparkled with such high spirit that all with one accord recognized her as the princess of Crete, Ariadne, daughter of Minos and grandchild of the Sun.

At a sign from her, Theseus approached. At another sign the others turned and retreated to an opening which still flamed with the lingering red of the west.

She, with still panting bosom and cheeks afire, smiled, her eyes half closed. Extending her fair arms, she drew aside the heavy, dark curls on the Hero's temples. . .

"Thou art comely," she said, happily.

He remained silent. Ignoring this, she resumed:

"Ah! Well I know that thou goest to slay the Minotaur and that all the Gods will lend their weight to thine arm when thou shatterest that wild, surly muzzle upon the stones. But how wilt thou come out from that inextricable crypt? Thou, in thy triumph, and holding aloft the repulsive head of the Monster, thou wouldst perish in the cunningly contrived corridors, between two walls always the same. And that which Strength should have accomplished, dull Forgetfulness would condemn to oblivion. Thou knowest not that this palace is a labyrinth of stone and that those who enter it cannot escape. But I have thought

[25]

of thee, son of Pandionian Ægeus, and, in the space between my breasts, I have brought thee refuge."

Her hand disappeared into her tunic and presently drew out a green ball.

"Look!" she said. "Here is my Miletian thread. It is as fine as one of my hairs and as long as the circuit of the island. With it I could weave green robes for all the nymphs of this forest, or a floating veil to cover the sea. Take it. Thou wilt unwind it all before reaching the distant retreat of the Monster. And it will lead thee back to the light."

She turned toward the victims.

"Go," she said, "You are saved."

They fled; except Myris, who did not move.

Theseus accepted the ball of thread and asked:

"Who art thou?"

"I am thine."

"But what shall I call thee?"

"I am called Ariadne, sevenfold daughter of Zeus by the grand-parents of my father who is Minos, King of Crete. But if another name pleases thee better, say it and it shall be mine."

As though he were seeking a haven, he looked long into Ariadne's eyes. Then, without another word, he entered the Labyrinth.

"Theseus! Theseus!" she called.

"Theseus, stop! I cannot wait; I want to go! I would watch thee! Oh, I am athirst

to assist in thy terrible victory! Together! I will carry the thread, and when thou hast overthrown the Beast I will kiss thy dear hands bruised by his horns, and thou shalt be my husband in the hour of thy triumph."

When she followed him into the Dedalian night, she fastened the pendant end of the green thread to a rock; but when she emerged, in the arms of the Hero, letting the thread run through her closed hand, the anchor which connected them with life was the poor body of Myris, strangled.

II

Between the forests and the sea.
Morning.
A little beach, rounded, pure and yellow.
Ariadne, sleeping on the Isle of Naxos,
awakened without opening her eyes, for she
wished to live over again all that had happened
since that first day when Theseus had brought
to birth within herself a second, unknown
Ariadne.

She saw again the cedars—the blades of sunlight—the entrance of the infernal edifice—
the white-clad victims—the Hero without
weapons or armour—the green thread—the
anchor—the pathway—the sharply-winding
circuits—the heartbreaking descent—the interminable ascent—the Monster—the slaver-
ing nostrils—the horns—the horrible great
hands—the short struggle—the blood-spat-
tered earth—the return through the shadows
—the worshipful sight of day—the dew upon
the tips of the grasses—the evening upon the
tops of the cedars—the leisurely journey—
the departure—the first dip of the vessel—the
fragrance of the sea—the colour of the night
—the freshness of the dawn—and the second
day—the second twilight—the arrival.

She had slept close to the Victor, side by
side with his glory, and she awakened in per-

fect felicity before the horizon of a life equally happy and certain.

She reached out her hand. It fell upon the dull earth. It searched, turned, and drew back, empty. Everywhere grass or sand or cold flowers or mud.

She called: "Theseus!"

She opened her eyes and her mouth, sprang up, lifted her two arms; and a terrified sweat started in her hair. He was neither beside her, nor before her, at her feet, nor in her arms. . .

She ran toward the sea. The vessel had left its moorings. Far away, half upon the sky and half upon the water, a little black bird was flying, the rapid ship which bore the fortune of Theseus, so far away that the eye could scarcely see it and a despairing cry would die before reaching it.

Madness! She walked into the sea, throwing her tunic upon the pebbles. The waves slapped against her shivering thighs. The water mounted to her belly.

She cried out:

"O Poseidon, King of the Glaucous Fields, Guardian of the Waters! Lift me up! bear me to him; he is my very soul. . ."

Poseidon heard, but was silent. An impetuous wave embraced the pleading Ariadne and threw her gently upon the thick moss. The vessel had vanished forever beyond the wall of the sea.

Then an uproar, a multitude, cries of adulation, crackling steps on the soil of the forests.

"Io! Evoë! Who is upon the road? Who is upon the road?"

Down the mountain came Bacchantes and Satyrs and Pans, the procession hurried along by the thyrses.

"Who is upon the road? Who is in the dwelling? Iacchos! Iacchos! Evoë!"

Their hands carried aloft branches of trees and garlands of ivy. Their hair was so burdened with blossoms that their necks bent backward; the folds of their breasts were rivulets of sweat, their thighs glowed like setting suns and their mouths were flaked with flying foam.

"Iacchos! Beautiful God! Mighty God! Living God! Iacchos! Leader of the Orgy! Iacchos! Impulse and Guide! Incite the multitude! Drive the rout and the rapid feet! We are thine! We are thy swelling breath! We are thy turbulent desires!"

Suddenly they caught sight of Ariadne.

They rushed upon her, seizing her arms and her legs, and twisting her disordered hair. The first grasped her head, and, bracing a foot on her shoulder, wrenched it off, like a heavy flower; others scattered the members; the sixth tore open the belly and pulled out the little womb; and the seventh, digging into the chest, uprooted the convulsive heart.

Then the God appeared!

They hurled themselves toward him, waving

their trophies.

He was naked and crowned with vine leaves. A fawn skin hung upon his loins. He carried a rod of box-wood. He said:

"Leave these poor members."

The Bacchantes threw them upon the ground and, impelled by a gesture, rushed off up the mountain, like a flock pursued by bees.

The God inclined his hollow rod which gushed out marvellously; and the members reunited, the heart awoke suddenly, and deluded Ariadne raised herself upon one hand. She said softly:

"O Dionysos!"

. . . .

Night lay over the sea, clear and sombre.

The God spread out his fingers, and said in a grave, tender tone:

"Arise! I am Awakening. Arise! I am Life. Give me thy hand. . . Come with me. . .

"This is the Pathway of Peace."

III

A high, bare ravine.
Night.
Peace.

"What happened?" asked Ariadne. "I no longer remember his name; yet I recall that he abandoned me."

"What happened," answered the God, "is the law of the love in which thou didst rely: he left thee. Those who demand shall not be loved; those who shall be loved shall go. And this is why thou didst deceive thyself. But today thou art upon the true road, upon the Pathway of Peace."

"What then, O King Dionysos, is this peace?"

"Thou dost not feel it?"

"Truly, I am no longer Ariadne. I no longer feel the stones nor the leaves which, at one time, bruised my feet. I no longer feel even the freshness of the air. I feel thy hand."

"Yet I am not touching thee."

"Where dost thou lead me, Adored God?"

"To where thou shalt never again see the sun too glittering nor the night too shadowy. To where thou shalt never again feel hunger nor thirst nor love nor fatigue. From the worst of evils, the fear of death, Ariadne, thou art delivered; for, in truth, thou art already dead. And, see, what happiness!"

[32]

"Ah! Could I but believe that one can be happy without pernicious Love."

"Look at me. . ."

"I see thee without it. I see thee. O Saviour! Where dost thou lead me?"

"To a land which is indeterminate, crepuscular, unvarying, colourless, airy. The grasses there are like the flowers, pale as the sky and the water. The air is always still; and the light is mysterious like a winter's day or a night of summer. One knows not whether day mounts over the earth or descends into the lower firmament. The buds never close, the petals no longer fall, there are no birds among the branches, and the uproar of six thousand million souls is a fathomless silence. Thou shalt have eyes no longer: what wouldst thou see? Thou shalt no longer have hands: what wouldst thou touch? No longer shalt thou have lips: thou shalt be delivered from the kiss. But the shadow of reality shall subsist about thee, the remnant of a dream without joy and without regret; without desire and without pleasure; thou shalt no longer taste sorrow."

"Dost thou also inhabit this land which thou dost promise me at last?"

"I am the Ruler of the Shades, the Spirit of the Infernal Water. I sit upon a throne of shadows; my upraised finger draws the souls to it and, from the farthest ends of the earth they come, whirling, yielding, beating their wings beneath my glance. I bear a coronal of vine leaves for, even as the cut grapes revive under the feet in the press and stream forth in scarlet wine, so the anguish of death is miraculously transfigured in the ecstasy of resurrection. And I carry in my hand a blade of ripe wheat for, as the corrupt grain is born again in the nurturing earth and sprouts forth in living herbage, so pain and trouble germinate, flower, become glorious, in the great eternal peace whither thou goest."

"Shall I be far from thee, a poor soul alone in the multitude?"

"No: thou shalt reign, thou also, at my side, O Queen with beautiful hair! And thou shalt reflect, on thy face, the ineffable calm of the subterranean fields. It is thou the dead souls shall see first, and thou shalt have this joy which is refused even to the Gods: that of seeing the birth of felicity in the forever-calm eyes of incorruptible Spirits."

"O Dionysos! . . ."

And her uplifted arms welcomed him joyously.

. . . . .

"Is that all?" asked Philinna.

"I shall say no more."

"But is not Persephone queen of the underworld!" Rhea demanded.

"Yes," said Thrases.

Then Melandryon, who had listened to the

end of the mythological tale, drew aside the narrator and, fixing him with a penetrating eye:

"Thou hast not told all that was in thy mind."

"No. When Dionysos had spoken thus to the daughter of Minos, the truth is that he destroyed her. But, by the mere prophecy of so glorious a future, had he not given her more joy than he promised her in it? I proceeded to do for these women what he did for Ariadne. Do not enlighten them. It is better to give confidence than to fulfil oaths, for hope is sweeter than conquest."

"Remembrance is sweeter than hope."

"Women do not think so."

THE HOUSE UPON THE NILE

or The Mask of Virtue

Amaryllis disposed herself indolently upon the velvet moss, and touched the youngest man's hand with the tip of her willow branch.

"Do thou relate something, Clinias," she said. "I would hear a story from thee."

But Clinias hesitated.

"I can repeat the legends which everyone knows; but I know not how to gild them, like Thrases, with the brush of novelty, nor how, like thee, Amaryllis, to enliven them by the witchery of words. I will tell, if permitted, what my friend Bion of Clazomenæ confided, on his return from Ethiopia."

"Is it a true happening?" asked Rhea.

"Yes. But I would have you accept it as a fable and believe that the personages are followed by the shadow of their symbol. If the power were mine, it would not be much trouble for me to make this short history a poem in hexametres; or perhaps simply to generalize it."

The hot glare of the sun above the tall forest made the fragrant coolness under the leaves the more grateful. Stray beams glinted caressingly upon Lampito, who had screened her face with her hair. Amaryllis reclined near Rhea. Philinna toyed with her hands. Melandryon gazed at the ground.

Then Clinias began this tale:

I

Bion had ascended the Nile above Thebes and Hermonthis, above Silsila and Ombos. He had passed even the Elephantine Isle where the territory of Egypt ends, and had advanced toward black Ethiopia which is close to the edge of the world.

He had no boat with which to conquer the slow roll of the river; for that he would have needed slaves, and he distrusted paid companions. He journeyed, then, on foot along the damp grassy banks which were so narrow that the path sometimes ran along the foot of multi-coloured cliffs from which stretched back the endless expanse of the Desert.

Between two dull solitudes swept this narrow band of vital earth, this road of flaming fields and of luxurious herbage, split to the two horizons by the luminous green of the Nile. Everywhere resounded the cries of birds, shrill and thronging: in the blue air, upon the moving water, under the tall grasses, and among the bare branches of the fat baobabs like perpetual, deafening locusts.

Over the distant wastes scampered ostriches and giraffes; herds of antelopes fled like yellow clouds; monkeys hung suspended in fantastic groups from the supple branches of the sycamores. And sometimes, in the mud of the Nile, where the slender steps of the ibises followed each other like long flowers, Bion was astonished to observe the formidable human imprint of that mysterious Amanit, the beast upon which no man dared look, but of which the Ethiopians had strange tales to relate. And Bion felt, in an uneasy way, that the Colossi of rose granite, sculptured in the mass of the mountains, assumed a nocturnal life and came to bathe themselves to the knees in the holy river, the provident father of all.

For the remains of Egyptian greatness still lingered in an impious land, even so far from Thebes and Memphis. Long since, the Autochthons had retaken the land from the conquerors, and yet the face of Rhameses was forever stamped upon the steep cliffs; for the rulers of the North had given their form to the rocks which the chisel of slaves had subdued but which neither time nor Zeus could erase.

It was winter. Night brought a cool mist which spread over the land. The dreamy days

were still oppressive. Bion searched out the
shade and the springs in the forests of mimosas
where lions withdrew from the sun to issue
only at the rising of the night. There also
lived the men, barricaded in their cabins behind palisades of date palms, where Bion was
a guest, night after night, until the early
morning summoned him forth.

II

Then one evening, as he had walked a long time under a painful radiance and his weary feet swelled under their narrow straps, he approached a house of brown and green raised alone on the bank of the Nile with dry mud and interwoven grasses. The heavy heads of many palms bent about it, and it was so overrun by large flowering water grasses that one might say it was floating upon the same water or at hazard in a marsh.

Resting for a moment, with his shoulder against a tree, Bion regarded the house.

There were two young girls disporting themselves on the threshold, talking and laughing. The elder wore a full, blue, fringed garment, gathered under the arms and falling to the bare knees. Her abundant dark hair was separated in a thousand thin strands closely framing a face with shining eyes and thick lips and falling only as far as the delicate, full shoulders. With her loins bent over a low bar, she laughed, and tossed her head.

The younger was still a child and of course wore nothing. She sat squatting upon her heels, her small head bent between her knees, and stuck little yellow flowers between her outspread toes.

Bion watched them interestedly, without

venturing nearer. He contemplated the House. Mysterious like any object beheld for the first time, it seemed guarded by its air of strangeness, solitude and uncertainty. People lived there. For how long a time? What sadnesses, what furtive happiness lurked in this hut of mud and branches? Whose hands had built it? Who had inhabited it? What deaths, what births, had it seen? He had the feeling that these mysteries were impenetrable and that this lost corner would never be known to him.

Evening fell swiftly, and at last Bion came up. Immediately the two girls drew back toward the open house, uttering little cries. But he did not approach them. He said, simply:

"I ask for shelter."

"Father is in the fields," explained the elder. "Wait until he returns and he will receive thee."

Bion again rested his arm against a tree and looked toward the Nile, annoyed by the curious glances which roamed about his person.

It was long after sunset when the Ethiopian arrived. He drove before him a yellow ox with tapering horns. When he drew near, the two girls burst at once into speech:

"A stranger is here.—He asks for shelter.— Yes, he is alone.—Over there, leaning against the tree.—We would not let him come in until thy return.—Have we done right, father?"

The master took three steps in the darkness and addressed Bion in a clear voice:

"You are welcome. Enter my house."

They entered the room which had been brightened by lamps of baked earth:

"Here is water, bread and fruits," said the Ethiopian.

They ate and drank in silence. The host felt that it would be indelicate to ask for explanations which had not been offered.

She of the brown body draped with blue served the food and poured water from the jars. The younger girl had drawn back against the earthen wall, and was considering the Stranger, her hands pressed over her mouth.

When they had eaten their full, the host arose.

"It is time to go to thy bed. I know the duties of hospitality. Here are my two daughters. The younger has not yet known a man but she is of an age to come to thee. Go, and take thy pleasure with her."

This custom was not unfamiliar to Bion and he respected it as a tradition of singular virtue. Did not the gods often visit the earth in the garb of travellers, soldiers or shepherds, and who could distinguish a mortal from an Olympian who did not wish to reveal himself? He, Bion, might be Hermes! A refusal, he knew, would be taken as an insult; thus he was neither surprised nor perturbed when the elder girl bent toward him and uncovered her young breasts so that he might kiss them.

Motionless and without uttering a syllable

[46]

the child watched their progress and poised herself, her head forward, her hands slack as though in a dream.

After an instant of paleness, trembling, on the verge of tears, she precipitated herself through the open door. The night swallowed her.

The father, raising his eyes, also walked to the threshold and peered into the sombre darkness where his younger child had carried away forever the good fame of his house.

III

The sun had risen when Bion awakened and took up his skin bag to continue his way. There was no one in the house when he left.

He was sorry not to see his Host, but felt no astonishment at not finding his companion of the night. She was too wise to expose herself to a farewell.

He resumed his journey.

The road he took beside the reeds of the Nile was so dazzling that he soon abandoned it for a little path which crossed the spongy fields toward the woods.

A sluggish hippopotamus had devastated a whole field of rice beneath his gross, purplish flesh, and lay amidst the ruin he had caused. Passing him quickly, Bion entered the shadow of the mimosas.

He was stopped suddenly by a cry of joy. So tender was it, so full of recognition, so expressive of p e r f e c t happiness, that Bion turned quickly with an involuntary smile.

He recognized the little fugitive, naked as on the night before, a little timid, but hopeful, and awaiting only a gesture from him to cast herself into his arms and weep for joy.

"It is thou! At last!" she cried. "I knew not where thou wouldst pass; not even whether thou wouldst go up the Nile. I only knew I would see thee again. I came here and I waited for thee. I divined well that thou wouldst turn away from the sun of the road and that thou wouldst go by the wood. Oh! How happy I am! It seemed to me that three days passed while I waited. . . I am no longer. . . That which has come to me is so extraordinary. . ."

And she added, more sadly:

"Thou didst remain a long time with her."

Bion stood motionless and gazed at her with some uneasiness.

"But, my little child, why didst thou come here?"

"Why?" she echoed. "I came to follow thee, to remain with thee always, always. . ."

"Thou comest to follow me, and yesterday, when thy father gave thee to me, thou didst flee like a foolish hare. I did not please thee last evening and I please thee this morning, for no reason? Thou behavest strangely."

The poor child heard him through, then suddenly pressing her little nude, sob-racked body against a tree, gave way to tears.

Bion detested touching scenes more than any other tiresome things. He tapped the child's shoulder with his finger, and said:

"Farewell. Return to thy father's house. He will be pleased.'"

And he left her, tranquilly.

But she ran quickly after him, and grasped him by the mantle, by the arm, by the neck, saying hurriedly:

[49]

"I shall go where thou goest, I loved thee yesterday as I do today; I had never loved anyone before; I love only thee, O, I shall love only thee. . . I ran off yesterday because I was jealous of my sister, because I could not share thee with her nor love thee before her. If I had not gone, thou wouldst have taken me in passing and left me forever. After thee I would have given myself to another and to another, and so on until my marriage. Knowest thou that my sister has already known more strangers than I could tell thee in opening my two hands seven times? And I, also, should I have done that? Oh, I have felt sure that, for all my life, I should belong to the same man, to the first who should take me. And thou art he! Take me, keep me always! I want to be thy wife and to follow thee."

Wearied, and wanting to be free, Bion replied:

"My dear girl, thou reasonest like a child. Thou sayest thyself that thou hast never loved anyone, and I am well convinced of it for, in the arms of her first lover, a woman already dreams of her second, and, in her heart, it is he whom she loves. Thou wilt soon learn this.

"What virtue is there in always loving the same man? Wouldst thou wish to sleep all thy life under the same roof? to wear always the same robe? to eat always the same fruit? Love is not a sensation so very different from others, but of all it is the most bountiful: it is for

[50]

this reason that it can be shared.

"The gods have spread upon thy lips a love generous enough to satisfy an e n t i r e army. Thou hast no right to deprive others of the pleasure they hope for from thee. When thy sister shall marry, thou wilt remain alone in thy father's house: then there will still pass travellers who long since will have left their own hearth and the bed sacred to their marriage. Wearied by the sun and the length of the road, they will be refreshed by thine attentions. Thou wilt be able to conjure away their fatigue and to leave, in their life, the remembrance of a happy hour.

"Thus, through the passage of the days, the diversity of loves, the promptness of farewells, thou wilt understand, little by little, that one is not bound by love; and thou wilt more wisely choose the man to whom thou wilt give thy life."

"Could I ever choose b e t t e r ? Art thou not. . ."

"Oh, undoubtedly. Without question I am the best, the only one, and thou art very certain of having found thy dream. Is it not this thou wert going to say? Ah well, see how thou hast deceived thyself, I should leave thee immediately afterwards, just as I left thy sister this morning. In the situation thou art in, it would be best for us to do nothing and to part friends. It is a deplorable choice that thou didst make. Try to forget it and go at once

[51]

without turning thy head. In the House upon
the Nile thou wilt find again thine afflicted
father, the family hearth and the images of the
Gods. Thou wilt find again thine elder sister
and she will teach thee that true virtue of
which thou wearest only the mask."

He kissed her on the cheek and resumed his
walk between the trees. But he had not yet
passed from sight beyond the great thickets of
yellow flowers when, for the third time, he
heard running steps and weeping behind him.

He turned in sudden anger:

"I forbid thee to follow me!"

"But I cannot leave thee. Do not drive me
away. I do not ask to be a wife since thou
refusest to love me. I beg thee, let me stay
near thee. I shall belong to thee. Make anything of me you wish. . . your slave. . ."

Coldly removing his girdle, Bion wrapped it
like drawers around the child's loins, hung his
filled sack, the gourd and the petasus upon her
naked shoulder and said to her indifferently:

"Go ahead."

. . . . .

This narrative created an unfavourable sensation, and the women were inclined to think
that Bion was an abominable man. This was
made much worse when Rhea, who always
wanted to know the final end of stories and
the disposition of all the characters, asked:

"And then what happened?"

Clinias concluded thus:

"Before the evening of the same day, Bion sold her to a wandering chief of the plains and he never heard what became of her."

The women murmured indignantly; but Thrases had already begun to speak:

"That was his obvious right. Had she not said to him: 'I belong to thee?' The privilege accompanying things which are owned is that they can be sold. There is nothing to say against it and, beside, she was a little fool whom he did well to pass over."

Melandryon was more severe:

"Reasons like that," he said, "are all too moral. Things cannot be judged by the relation of Good and Evil. These are considerations which vary with climate and chronology, and of which the importance is much exaggerated. The single rule of life which seems valid is the preservation of beauty. If the child was pretty (Clinias did not tell us this) Bion committed a grave fault in selling her to a stupid negro who would brutalize the charm of her form and the grace of her movements."

"Her nose was very broad," responded Clinias, "her lips heavy, and her skin brown."

"In that case," said Melandryon, "he could not of course be expected to concern himself."

BYBLIS

or The Miracle of Tears

Amaryllis, stretched at her ease between the three young women and the three philosophers, poured into their receptive ears as into those of little children, the following fabulous tale:

"It was from travellers who had pressed farther along the Meander than anyone had ever gone before, and who had been in Caria, that I heard about the God of the sleeping river: how they had seen him, and listened to his drowsy voice, as he emerged at nightfall, crowned with rushes, his wrinkled face shadowed by a long green beard, like the grasses that hang from the grey banks. His immortal eyelids seemed dead as they drooped over eyes forever sightless. Those who would seek him today would probably call in vain upon his spirit to reveal itself.

"Now he it was whose love for the nymph Cyanis bore fruit in Byblis, the unhappy one, whose story you shall hear."

I

In the secret grotto from which the river mysteriously issued, the nymph Cyanis brought forth two children at one birth: one was a boy whom she named Caunos, the other a girl, Byblis.

Together they grew up on the banks of the Meander, and sometimes their mother showed them, under the light upon the surface, the divine image of their father whose spirit moved the swelling waters.

Of the world that stretched beyond their forest birthplace, they knew nothing. They had never seen the sun except reflected fitfully through the leafy branches. Byblis never left her brother, and when they walked together her arm was lovingly twined about him.

Her mother had woven for her in the depths of the water a little tunic which she always wore; it was blue and gray like the first appearance of the dawn. Caunos wore only a girdle of rushes about his loins from which hung a yellow cloth.

When the day had gilded a path for them in the wood, they would roam far off together, gathering the fallen fruits or searching for the largest flowers and those which breathed the rarest perfume. The discoveries of one were always for the other also, and they never quarreled. Because of this their mother boasted of them to the other nymphs who were her friends.

Now, when twelve years from the day of their double birth had passed over their heads, Cyanis became uneasy and sometimes followed them.

For the two children no longer played; and, after spending a whole day in the forest, would return empty-handed, bringing neither birds nor flowers nor fruits nor garlands. They walked so closely together that their hair mingled. The girl's hands would wander over her brother's arms, and sometimes she would kiss him on the cheek. Then they would both remain silent.

When the heat wearied them too much, they would creep in among the low branches, where the moss was most fragrant, and there lie upon their breasts, talking together, ad-

miring each other, closely entwined.

Then Cyanis called her son to her and asked him:

"Why art thou sad?"

To this the boy replied:

"But I am not sad. In former times, I laughed and played. Now all is greatly changed. I have no need of games, mother, and if I no longer laugh it is because I am happy."

Cyanis asked:

"Why art thou happy?"

And Caunos replied:

"I look at Byblis."

Cyanis persisted:

"Why dost thou no longer care for the forest?"

"Because the hair of Byblis is softer than the grasses, and more sweet to smell; because the eyes of Byblis. . ."

But Cyanis cried:

"Child! Be silent!"

Hoping to cure him of his forbidden passion, she took him at once to the dwelling of a mountain nymph who had seven daughters whose beauty was more than words could describe. And the two mothers, concerting together, charged him:

"Choose the one who pleases thee, Caunos; she shall be thy wife."

But Caunos looked at the seven marvellous young creatures with an eye as cold as though he saw seven rocks; for his little soul was filled with the image of Byblis and he had no place in him for an unknown tenderness.

For a month, Cyanis conducted her son thus from mountain to mountain and from diversion to diversion, but without once succeeding in luring him from his dream.

Divining at last that she was powerless to influence this passionate obstinacy, she began to dislike her son and to taunt him with infamy. But he did not understand at all why he was thus upbraided. Why, among all women, should he be denied the very one he loved? Why should the tenderness which would be permitted in the importunate arms of another become criminal in the adored arms of Byblis? For what unknown reasons should a feeling which he knew to be tender and good, capable of any sacrifice, be judged worthy only of every punishment?

"Zeus," he thought, "had certainly espoused his sister; and Aphrodite Dionæa, with her brother Ares, had dared to deceive her brother Hephæstos." For he did not yet know that the gods had given intelligent morality only to themselves and that they troubled virtue with incomprehensible laws.

And Cyanis finally said to her son:

"I renounce thee as my child."

She stopped a centauress on her way to the sea and forced Caunos to mount astride her.

The great beast galloped away like the wind. Cyanis followed them with her eyes for some

time. Caunos, frightened, sometimes blinded
by the masses of flying hair, held fast to the
shoulders of the centauress. She galloped with
long, powerful bounds, following a straight
line, until she diminished in the green distance.
Then she was hidden by a clump of trees, from
which she quickly emerged, but smaller, like a
dot which hardly seemed to move. At last
Cyanis could no longer distinguish her.

Slowly Byblis' mother turned her steps
toward the forest. She was sick at heart, but
proud also, at having saved, by a violent sep-
aration, the destinies of her children; and she
thanked the gods for having strengthened her
to accomplish the painful duty.

"Now," she thought, "Byblis, left alone,
will forget her absent brother. She will listen
to the first one who speaks words of love to
her, and, perhaps, a line of demi-gods will issue
from the bed of an orderly marriage. Blessed
are the immortal gods!"

But when she returned to the grotto, she
found no one. Little Byblis was no longer
there.

II

Byblis, finding herself alone on the little bed of green leaves where she had always slept with her brother, courted sleep in vain; no dreams soothed her anxiety, which found vent instead in hideous visions.

She arose; the night was calm and sweet. A slow respiration lifted the profound masses of the forest. She seated herself upon a stone and gazed long at the gliding water.

"Caunos," she thought, "Caunos. Why has he not come back to me? What attraction can detain him? Oh, why has my brother left me?"

Suddenly she leaned over the spring, and said in a low ardent voice:

"My father! My father! Where is Caunos? Tell me. . ."

A murmur of the waters answered her:

"Far. . ."

Startled, Byblis went quickly on:

"And he will come back? When will he return?"

"Never. . ." replied the spring.

"Oh! Is he dead!"

"No. . ."

"Where shall I find him?"

". . ."

The murmuring voice was silent. The light rustling of the reeds was heard again, mo-

notonously. No divine image stirred the pure
waters.

Byblis raised herself, and ran. She knew the
path Caunos and her mother had taken. It
was a narrow passage which wound among the
trees and submerged itself in the forest. She
did not often follow it because it crossed a
low ground which was infested with serpents
and evil beasts. But this time her desire was
stronger than her fear and she hurried on,
trembling, at the best speed of her little, naked
feet.

The night was not dark; but the shadows
from the moon were black and, among the
largest trees, Byblis had to feel her way.

When she came to a place where the path
divided, she paused. How should she know
which road to take? Dropping to her knees,
she searched the ground for a long time in
the hope of a guiding mark. The ground was
dry. Byblis could see nothing. But, as she
raised her head, she saw, half hidden among
the leaves of an oak, a hamadryad with green
breasts, who watched her, smiling.

"Tell me!" cried Byblis. "Which way did
he take? If thou didst see him, tell me. . ."

The hamadryad extended one of her long,
branch-like arms toward the right. Byblis,
rising, thanked her with a grateful look.

She walked for a long time that night. The
path stretched on, scarcely visible under the
fallen leaves; winding always, according to

the ground and the trees, rising, descending, interminably in the darkness.

Weighted by weariness at last, Byblis sank upon the moss, and slept.

She awakened next day, under a sun which was already high, to a strange soft sensation along her extended hand. When she opened her eyes, she saw that a yellow hind was licking it, slowly. But at her first involuntary movement, the delicate animal bounded upon its slender hooves, raised its two ears, and fixed upon her its beautiful, humid eyes which were dark and gleaming like water among the rocks.

"Hind," said Byblis, "whose art thou? If thou belongest to the goddess Artemis, guide me, for I know her. When the full moon floats through the forest, I give her libations of goat's milk. She knows this, hind, and loves me well. If thou art one of her followers, deliver me from my suffering, and be sure that thy good deed will not displease the kind Huntress of the Night."

The hind seemed to understand. She walked slowly forward, spacing her steps so that the child could follow her.

Thus they crossed together a great part of the forest and also two brooklets which the hind leaped at a bound but which Byblis could pass only by entering water up to her knees. Byblis was now full of confidence. She felt sure that she was on the right road. Might not the goddess herself have sent this hind, as

a reward for her devotion? And the divine
animal would guide her across the wood to the
well-beloved brother whom she would never
leave again. Each step seemed to bring her
nearer to Caunos. Exultantly, she already felt
against her breast the affectionate embrace of
her lost one. His remembered breath seemed to
have passed in the air, enchanting the fragrant
breeze.

Suddenly, the hind stopped. She slipped her
young head between two slender trees where,
at that moment, appeared the horned profile
of a stag. And, as though she had accomplished
her desired end, she lay down, her hoofs under
her belly, and rested her chin upon the grass.

Byblis called:

"Caunos! Caunos, where art thou?"

Her only reply was a sudden movement
in her direction by the stag, whose terrible
threatening horns were twisted like ten tawny
reptiles. Then Byblis understood that like herself, the hind had been in quest of her lover;
and that it is perhaps useless to depend on the
good offices of those who are already fully possessed by an intimate passion.

She turned back only to find that she was
lost. She tried a new path which swooped
down toward an invisible valley. Her poor
naked feet bruised by the stones, pierced by
the sharp roots, slipped on the brown carpet
of pine needles. At a turn of the irregular
path, which followed the course of a brook,

she came upon a divine couple. Two nymphs of different essences, one lived in the forest and the other in the water of springs. The oread had brought the naiad fresh offerings received from humans, and they bathed together in the stream, undulating and enlaced.

Byblis addressed one of them:

"Naiad," she said. "Hast thou seen the son of Cyanis?"

"Yes. His shadow passed over me yesterday, at sundown."

"From whence did he come?"

"I know not."

"Whither did he go?"

"I did not see."

Byblis' disappointment quivered in a long sigh.

"And thou," she said, to the other nymph, "Hast thou seen the son of Cyanis?"

"Yes. Far from here, upon the mountain."

"From whence did he come?"

"I know not."

"Whither did he go?"

"I have forgotten."

Then, raising herself amidst the rapid waters:

"Stay with us, young maid," she said. "Why dost thou dream still of one who is with thee no longer? Infinity has stored up for you a world of present joys. The future has nothing to offer that is worth the trouble of pursuing."

But Byblis did not believe her in the least.

Although she could not have expressed herself so well, her little soul could conceive of no rest, no joy, except in persevering in her search for perfect happiness. During the first day of her hopeless pilgrimage, she had relied on the aid and interest of unknown friends. Since she had seen them indifferent toward her purpose, she no longer counted on anyone but herself. And, leaving the winding path, she plunged fearlessly into the labyrinth of the wood.

The wise words of the two immortals followed her like a refrain:

"Stay with us, young maid. Why dost thou dream still of one who is with thee no longer? The future has nothing to offer that is worth the trouble of pursuing."

And long, long after, the child, climbing higher and higher up the mysterious mountain, heard in the distance two clear voices crying in unison:

"Byblis! Byblis!"

III

All that night and all the next day, Byblis wandered over the mountain. Eagerly she questioned all the divinities of the woods, of the trees, of the glades, and of the shadowy caves. She poured out her sorrow in little gushes of confidence, she supplicated, she trembled, she wrung her little hands. But no one had seen Caunos.

Now she had climbed so far that the sacred name of her mother was no longer known where she passed, and the strange nymphs did not understand her words.

She wished to retrace her steps, but she had lost herself. A giant colonnade of pines walled her in. There were no more paths scratched in the grass. There was no horizon. She ran here and there, futilely. She called with desperate hope.

There was no longer even an echo.

Then, as her weary eyelids were closing, little by little, she lay down upon the ground, and a passing dream said to her, in slow solemn tones:

"Thou wilt never see him again, thy brother; thou wilt never see him again."

She awakened with a deadly fear upon her.

Her hands stretched out, her lips parted, but no sound came; she had not the strength to give vent to her anguish.

A blood-red moon had risen behind the black wall of the pines. Byblis could scarcely see it. A moist veil seemed to have spread itself over her dark eyes. All around her an eternal silence slumbered.

And then a strange moisture gathered in the corner of her left eye.

Byblis had never wept. She believed now that she was going to die, and she sighed with relief to feel the mysterious solace that stole over her.

The tear spread, trembled, and flooded the orb. Then suddenly it rolled refreshingly over her cheek. Byblis remained motionless, her eyes fixed, beneath the blood-red moon. And then a swollen tear filled the corner of her right eye. It enlarged like the first, slipped through the lashes, and fell.

Two other tears were born of these, two burning drops which left damp paths on her cheeks. They reached the corners of her mouth; a delicious bitterness enervated the stricken soul.

So, never again should her hand touch the affectionate hand of Caunos. Never again should she see the shadowy glow of his gaze, his loved head, his soft young hair. Never again should they dream, side by side, entwined upon the same bed of leaves. The forests had even forgotten his name.

A crisis of despair shook her and her face

sank into her two hands. But such floods of tears swept over her burning cheeks that she felt as though a miraculous spring were bearing away all her sufferings, like dead leaves upon the waters of a torrent.

The tears rose gently within her, mounted to her eyes, swam, overflowed, and, gliding in a warm stream over her cheeks, inundated her narrow breast and fell upon her close-joined legs. But she did not feel them now rounding, one by one, between her long eyelids: they had merged into a smooth, continuous stream, an inexhaustible flow, the effusion of a divine consolation.

Meanwhile, awakened by the moonlight, the immortals of the forest had hastened up from all sides. The bark of the trees had become transparent, revealing the forms of the nymphs; and even the glistening naiads, leaving their waters and their rocks, had joined their playfellows in the wood.

They clustered about Byblis, pleading with her in terror, because of the steady flow of tears that had marked, in the earth, a deep sinuous line which moved slowly toward the plain.

But Byblis no longer heard anything, neither voices, nor steps, nor the night wind. Little by little, her posture became eternal. Cleansed by the tears, her skin had taken the smooth, white tint of marble bathed by the waters. Her hair no longer stirred along her arms at the wind's breath. Her grief had carved its symbol in pure stone. A shadowy light still flickered dimly in her vision. Suddenly, this went out; but the fresh tears still ran unceasingly.

. . . .

"It was thus that Byblis was changed into a fountain."

DANÆ

or Unhappiness

The day was so beautiful that the sadness bred by the story of the night before had melted with the mist. The buoyancy of Spring bent the branches of the trees and made the fields overflow along the narrow paths.

The women ran about in the wood; their laughter filtered through the trees. The full-blown flowers, seeking to detain their steps, empurpled the edges of the tunics. A sea of violets bathed the feet of the cedars. And here the young people lay down in a circle.

Now, as the hour had struck to summon the divine spirits that guard the forests, Rhea, a straightforward young girl, for whom words had no profound significance, thought to interpret the mood of all by demanding of Thrases "a story about happiness."

"Oh, yes," cried Lampito.

"No, oh, no!" exclaimed Amaryllis, "not that, above all! One should never speak of happiness. He who reveals his happiness, squanders it, word by word. He who tells of the happiness of others, uncovers his own sorrow. It is a story of pain which I shall tell you today. Unhappiness gives birth to pity, which is gentle and beneficent. In the unhappiness of Danæ each of you shall recognize your own, and you shall become glad with the remembrance of lost sorrows."

Wordlessly, the others grouped themselves about her and listened as she related this fable:

I

When Danæ, the mother of Perseus, left the Argonian shores, she remained for a long while at the stern, looking after the land that gradually drew back from the lengthening stretch of waters.

Her father had placed her, naked, in a long, black boat with her new-born child, and two little funereal oboli, so that she could pay her own and her son's passage on that other boat when the night of death should have filled their eyes, through famine, cold, or the tossings of the sea.

There was neither mast nor sails, but the brisk wind hastened the passage of the light, hollow b a r g e. A gull with curved wings followed it for some time in uncertain flight, then returned, weary-winged, toward the land. Danæ felt that she was now quite alone, and, pressing her hands over her eyes, she gave way to tears.

But she did not weep long, for into her simple soul grief had not yet penetrated. At a little cry from her child, she turned, already smiling. She took him in her arms, lay at full length upon a woollen rug which covered the bottom of the boat, and began to play.

She held the child like a wax doll, amused by his great round eyes, his toothless mouth which tried to speak, the rosy folds of his wrists, and his nails which were so tiny that they might have been the wings of flies.

With quick tenderness, she nearly crushed him in her arms; she caressed his little bald head, his little legs, his little doubled-up feet; she made him walk upon her, jump, run, fall, roll. She enveloped him in her hair, and, with a finger on his lip, she made him laugh.

At last she tired of her game:

"Listen," she said to him. "I will relate thy history."

It was not probable that the child could understand her. Nevertheless, he was of a divine race and nothing was impossible for those born of the great Olympians.

His mother spoke to him thus:

"I am Danæ, the daughter of Acrisios who is king over the land of Argos. My mother is the wise Eurydice, and I have no brother with winged arrows, and no sisters with ringlets of violets.

"When I was a little girl, I remember having played on the banks of the Inachos, where Artemis was said to bathe; and in the forests of the Artemision where she hunted the yellow hinds. I had friends; I had slaves; when I passed in the streets, women stretched out their hands toward me. Then, suddenly, I was imprisoned, and I could no longer see either the water or the earth.

"I was locked in a bronze tower, so high that I could not hear even the uproar of the festivals of Dionysos. And the ceiling of my chamber was made of brazen bars, between which I could see the sky.

"It was there that I grew up, alone with my nurse, between the sky and the rugs. And as the years passed I forgot the earth and the wind among the trees and the colour of the water. I saw only the sky; but what an eventful thing is the sky! When I woke up in the morning, it was like a red curtain strewn with little green flowers. Clouds were born, grew, floated, mingled or scattered. Sometimes, before they disappeared, I gave them names; but they were the friends of a moment and, like a cup of wine thrown into a river, they dissolved in the driving wind. Behind them, the sky shone very clear and, around the sun, almost white, or rather a colour for which I had no name: the colour of light."

The baby commenced a soft wailing. She rocked him. He became quiet.

"When evening came, the sky was a great sapphire sea in which the outspread clouds

[81]

bathed themselves, like beautiful women with fair hair and yellow scarfs. At night, there were the stars.

"It was from above, it was from the distant sky, that there descended into me the miraculous rain. . ."

A smile stole over her face and she closed her eyes to recapture an idle remembrance. When she opened them again, the child was asleep. So she did not finish her story: how her inexplicable pregnancy had suddenly reawakened the senile fears of Acrisios to whom a diviner had predicted that he should die at the hand of his grandson. She did not tell how, for forty weeks, she had felt growing within her the seed of that marvellous love; nor how, with the child born into the world, the king now exposed them, she and he, to death by famine, by cold, or by the tossings of the sea.

But she did not need to think of that. Had not the miraculous power, which had brought about the birth of Perseus, saved her from the first peril, and was it not one's duty always to bow to the mandates of the gods?

The child awakened, moved his arms, and began to cry. She recalled that she had not nursed him since morning. Bending over him, she gave him her breast. The heat was suffocating. Danæ feared that the strong light would trouble the poor little body, and, for the second time, she screened his face with her thick soft hair.

Time rolled on, slowly, like the waters. Argos and Tiryns had disappeared. On the right hand and the left, the shores of the gulf stretched to the horizon, vaguely blended with the floating mists. In the distance a swift dolphin shot clear of the water, plunging in again head first. Sometimes green sea-wrack fastened itself around the prow, its two ends threading out in a doubled wake. Danæ detached it with her hand, wondering whether the wet strands which she held between her fingers had not served as a coronal on the forehead of some sea god.

Evening. There were no sails upon the sea. The sun was eclipsed by a resplendent cloud from which arose a wide shaft of light which seemed to issue from the waters. An infinite shadow hid the blue Ægean. The waves softened as though overtaken by drowsiness. The little boat scarcely moved: Danæ was not sure that it had not stopped. . . Then the wind fell, suddenly.

Danæ, who had laid down the child, took him up in her arms to nurse him again. But she had forgotten that she herself had eaten nothing since morning. Her milk was nearly exhausted: the child began to cry.

Danæ stared at him, then at her drooping breasts, and at the wide sea. Nothing frightened her about the sea except the awful silence; she shivered. On all the horizon she saw no living thing. The world seemed to have disappeared, leaving her utterly desolate. She dipped her hand along the side of the boat: even the water was motionless.

She tried to sing, but she no longer recognized her voice and fell suddenly silent.

Then she wept: she stretched out in the bottom of the boat where she could see only the changing sky, as in her room in the tower. And thus sleep overcame her.

II

Night lifted in the west, like a blue vapour, exuding here and there little bright drops of stars. The sea had become so calm that it reflected the wavering glimmer, and the little boat seemed suspended in the centre of a celestial sphere.

Then figures appeared in the mirror, disturbing its smooth tranquillity; and, if Danæ had not been asleep, she would certainly have trembled with fright. A hand emerged from the water. Not like the hands of the women of earth, for it was blue on the back, with a palm the colour of gold, as though it had caressed the sun plunged beneath the sea.

This hand lifted and grasped the edge of the boat; the entire arm appeared and then, floating on the water, the first ringlets of green hair; then the watery eyes and the mouth and the glistening body arose. This personage was the soft-cheeked Pherusa, one of the divine Nereids.

She took the child in her arms, not to steal him away but to save his life; for she placed between his lips the extended tip of her cool breast, and the child sucked and was filled.

After her appeared the faultless Evagora, not less beautiful and with equally graceful hands and arms, born, like her, of old Nereus and the fair-haired Doris. In her hand she bore a swaddling-band of bright purple with which she clothed the divine infant, so that the deadly breath of the night should not descend until the hour fixed in the shadowy dwellings beneath the earth.

Arose, after these, kind Antonoë who, in her turn, took the child and cradled him upon the waters. Then Nossa and Cymothoe, Actinia and Protomedia, all four irreproachable; and these bore with them from the depths of the sea, a bowl, so wide and so gleaming that the hardiest divers have never gazed on anything comparable to it. And Psamathis, too, appeared, she of the transparent hands, and Melita of the green nails and Thalia of the rosy ears. And these took up the sleeping Danæ and laid her in the wide-spreading bowl upon a bed of soft sea-wrack and flowers from beneath the sea.

Then Protia, who excelled all her sisters in swimming, and Eucrata of the tender lips, and Saia, who blew the conch-shell, and Speia, who pursued the dolphins, pulled down the stern of the boat so that the sterile sea entered and, with a swirl, swallowed it up. Now all the other Nereids emerged suddenly. Eratia, who cast over the sea the petals of the rose of twilight; Eunica, whose hair under the water checked the swift ships; Amphitrite, whose bright eyes glistened in the hollows of green waves; Galenis, who could smooth out the billows; Pontoporia, who agitated the waters; Nesais, who appeared as an island to the voyagers from the west; Themistia, who carried away the star Iryllis and set it in a ring for her white toe; Cymatolegia, who gathered and drank the frothy foam; Lysianassa, ruler of the bottomless depths of the ocean; Hippothoë, who let the black ships pass between her naked legs without being touched by the highest masts; and Doris and Halimeda, who held each other by the hand; Evarne of the long eyelashes and light-fingered Agava.

When they were all united there, like a great cloud hovering about the moon-like bowl, the Old Man of the Sea appeared before them: Nereus, crowned with sea-wrack, the immortal who had generated this splendid race of Goddesses.

At a sign from him, the procession of his daughters followed; and, floating in their midst, he carried along the bowl, filled with glaucous light, where white-limbed Danæ slept with the infant Perseus, snatched from the insatiable deep.

The emergence of divine figures went on unceasingly. Proteus appeared, with his monstrous seals, born of the beautiful Halosydnis; Atlas, who was to be vanquished by the child; Thaumas, the dazzling spouse of Electra— father of the blue-eyed Iris and of the three virgin Harpies; Ino-Leucothea, who suffered immortality for love of her son, Melicertes;

Glaucos, who loved Scylla; Charybdis, dangerous to sailors; and Phorcys, god of storms and
of drowning.

Even the most terrible of these immortals
grew calm as they pressed shoreward, bearing
the fair young girl wrapped in her dream. The
dusky throng of the Tritons, heavy-lipped and
with calloused hands, swam more gently than
a school of little fish. They had stuffed the
twisted mouths of their conch-shells with sea-
weed, so that even the breeze of morning
would not vibrate in a distant rumour; and
they struck forward as cautiously as though
they feared that the waves, when parted,
would emit sound.

The wake of this marvellous multitude
stretched out to the two horizons.

III

When Danæ awoke, the child was nestling upon her bosom, and she herself lay upon a royal bed of purple byssus. At her first questions, she was told that the divinities of the sea had brought her to the Isle of Seriphos, and that she was now in the palace of Polydectes, the newly crowned king.

She lived there with her growing son, attending to him, spinning wool and gathering roses. Her life was happy and tranquil. Still faithful to the memory of the magic Gold, she had refused the hand of the king. She talked with no one except her old nurse, who had come from Argos to rejoin her and who was with her constantly.

The child grew. Twelve years passed by. He had been given a bow and arrows, and a small, sharp sword. He now passed all his days in the chase, alone, and sometimes lost himself in the vast forest swarming with beasts, some of which were divine. He accomplished miraculous conquests in those sombre thickets.

One evening, he returned, panting, dripping with perspiration and spattered with blood; two goat's feet protruded from his quiver. When he saw Danæ, he cried out:

"A good hunt, mother! All day I ran in the wood, pursuing this insolent little satyr who, the day before yesterday, mocked my bare lip and my pale legs. I followed his tracks in the damp earth and on the rocks scratched by his hoofs; and I met him at the entrance of his cave. I cast my bow from me and grappled with him, body to body. He was strong, mother; I smothered in his clasp. But I seized my bundle of arrows and, with one thrust, I buried them in his lean side. He gave a great cry and fell upon the grass like a wounded boar. Then I cut off these two hoofs which I bring to thee as a trophy."

Danæ shuddered at the child's cruelty, and the old nurse hid her eyes; for she saw, in this needless crime, the presage of a great misfortune to come. And, in truth, the fatal event occurred the day following.

Danæ had been given the liberty of the gardens, of all the palace, and all the riches of Polydectes, except one path, one door, one small enclosure.

For long years, she had wondered about the perpetual interdiction of this one point of the earth, and she had arrived at the belief that the little closed vault held, for her alone, all the happiness she did not possess, all the unknown joys which she desired more than life. On that day she ventured upon the path.

She opened the door.

She descended the first flight of stairs.

The second.

She reached the bottom.

Her old nurse came hastening to recall her, crying:

"Danæ! Danæ! Thou dost wrong to come here. Do not persist, Danæ! Thou hast been protected, as well thou knowest. Why wilt thou hasten to that from which thou art protected? There is but one place in the world where thou shouldst not go, and it is that which thou wouldst see. . . Thou wouldst not go out, thou wouldst not leave thy chamber except when the sun had set or when a storm thundered. Thou wouldst not go to other cities. No one ever saw thee in the fields. Thou wouldst never have come here, thou wouldst never have wished to, if I had not told thee that Polydectes had forbidden thee. Oh, why did I tell thee! Why did I speak when thou didst ask nothing? I am sure that this will bring thee harm. Still, once more, hear me, Danæ. I know why thou needest protection from what thou wouldst do today. I could not tell thee, but I know, I know, I know! It is concerned with thy happiness, I swear to thee by thy lovely hair which I saw lengthen, by thy lovely eyes which I often put to sleep, by thy lovely mouth which I nourished when thou lay curled in my arms like a little naked Eros.

"Danæ! Danæ! Do not descend these steps, do not fall into a snare, do not open the doors here, do not touch the locks nor turn the keys of bronze! It is thine unhappiness which is there: it is the sorrow of thy life. When one

knows one's sorrow, it should be forever forgotten! When one knows it not, one should
not search for it. Danæ! return, put out thy
lamp, return to the bright day, go away from
here, never return here, never think of it again.
Here thou goest toward doom, here thou goest
toward the darkness. . ."

Danæ spoke, in a slow voice:

"The oil—it has spilled upon my hands; it
has dropped upon my naked foot. I tremble.
Dost thou see, nurse? Take my lamp, I can
no longer carry it. Oh, I am impregnated with
its scent. I should have poured it all upon my
hands. But we have need of the lamp. Light
me, nurse."

Weeping, the nurse moaned:

"She enters; it was her destiny that she
should do so. It was her destiny that she should
know unhappiness. Oh, merciful gods! have
pity on us."

Danæ replied:

"I know something of what is behind this
door. Sorrow is always the same thing: a by-
gone joy which cannot be tasted again. . ."

And she continued, speaking as though in
a dream:

"What joy have I ever had to equal this
one? For I know well what is coming. That
is . . . I do not know all, but I apprehend something of it. Raise the light higher, nurse. I
am going to open the door."

"This is not even the door of a tomb. It is

something even more horrible. . . It is . . . but I cannot tell thee. Thou shalt see it, Danæ. It is thy destiny, as thou thyself canst see. No one can prevent thee. Thou couldst not prevent thyself from going in here."

"The door does not resist. The hinges are smooth. It must be often opened, this door, is it not? How is it that another should forbid me to enter where he passes freely? Or have the gods appointed that it is a misfortune for me alone and a happiness for all others?—The door gives way. I barely touched it with the tip of my finger and I felt it turn of itself. . . Seest thou, now, seest thou? Seest thou?. . ."

A shower of gold pieces rolled about her, through the wide opened door. She cried out in her fright:

"Ah! . . . Zeus . . . oh! oh! oh! . . . My lover!"

She threw herself upon the ground, in the midst of the glittering mass.

"Alas! Alas!" said the nurse. "Alas! It has come."

Danæ threw aside her tunic, her girdle, her embroidered ribbons.

"Zeus, my adored one! My Beloved! Oh, Tender Zeus! Then I meet thee again and, as before, in a prison of bronze. It was thee they concealed in this subterranean night, thunder-hurtling God! They set me free, and walled thee up, to let me die in the sunlight, ignorant of the hiding-place of thy splendour through which Perseus was magnified in my womb! Lover! Adored One! I am here! Awaken! Quicken thyself! Arise! Dost thou not know me? It is I, Danæ! Danæ."

Again and again she grovelled in the icy heap of gold pieces.

"Thou dost not hear me? . . . Oh, how cold thou art! It is as if my hands were plunged in snow . . . Ah! . . . Ah! it falls back . . . it no longer knows me. This is not he, nurse! . . . Tell me that this is not he. . . I had well divined this which has happened. . . Nurse, I cannot see any more. . . My arms are hurting. . .."

The nurse said to her:

"Danæ, come, we shall go up at once. We should not remain any longer in this place."

A NEW PLEASURE

I

It was four or five years ago, I remember, that I occupied, several days a week, a modest, quiet, well appointed ground floor, in a street that communicated at one end with the little Monceau Park. This last detail had little interest for me, because the gate was always closed in the evening before midnight, thus prohibiting me from walking there precisely at the hour when I most enjoyed the open air.

One night, finding myself at home, in silent company with two blue pottery cats crouched upon a white table, I meditated upon the charms of two possible ways of occupying my solitude: should I write a sonnet and smoke cigarettes—or smoke and write no sonnet, but gaze idly at the ceiling?

The really essential thing is always to have

a cigarette at hand; its smoke surrounds objects with a dreamy, celestial tint which softens lights and shadows, effaces sharp angles and, by a perfumed sorcery, confers upon the restless spirit a variable balance from which it can fall into reverie.

This evening it was my purpose to write and my desire to do absolutely nothing. The evening, then, seemed likely to resemble many others, fated to end before a virgin sheet of paper and an ash-tray full of cadavers, when I was roused from my indecision by an unexpected ring at the bell.

Startled, I entered upon a rapid calculation, and satisfied myself that, on Friday the ninth of June, at this hour of the night, I expected no one; but, when a second ring followed closely on the first, I walked to the door and drew the lock.

A woman stood on the threshold.

She was enveloped in a flowing cloak of woollen cloth like a traveller's cape, but woven in curious figures like an evening wrap. This was closed about her neck with a tufted roll of chenille from which her head barely emerged, brown under her blonde-tinted hair. Her young, sensual, slightly mocking face possessed as its most striking features, two very dark eyes, and a curved red mouth.

"Wilt thou permit me to enter?" she asked, her head inclining to one side in an appealing, yet confident manner.

[98]

I stepped aside with the pardonable astonishment of a man who sees entering his rooms, at an hour when he scarcely receives even his most intimate friends, a woman whom he could not recall ever having seen before and who, nevertheless, with her first words, addressed him familiarly as "thou."

"My dear lady," I said diffidently, when I had closed the door behind us, "Do not be angry with me for the remissness of my memory. I recognize thee, certainly, but by some singular default I cannot at the moment recall thy name. Is it, perhaps, Lucien? or Tototte?"

Her smile forgave my foolishness as, without responding, she laid aside her cloak. She was disclosed in a robe of water-green silk, embellished with huge irises woven into the cloth itself, the stems ascending along the body to the low, square-cut opening which left exposed the tops of her breasts. On each arm she wore a little golden serpent with emerald eyes. A necklace of large pearls in two rows shone upon her dark skin, defining the base of her rounded, mobile throat.

"If indeed thou dost recognize me," she said, "it is because thou has seen me in some dream. For I am Callisto, daughter of Lamia. For eighteen hundred years my tomb remained in peace in the flowery woods of Daphne, near the hills where once flourished voluptuous Antioch. Since then the tombs have travelled.

I was carried away to Paris and my shadow followed the stone which contained my fragile ashes. For a long time after, I slept in the glacial caverns of the Louvre. I might have remained there forever, if a noble pagan, a holy man, M. Louis Menard, who alone in this day remembers the divine rites and ceremonies, had not pronounced before my tomb the traditional words which restore to the unhappy dead an ephemeral and nocturnal life. For seven hours each night I can walk in thy squalid city. . ."

"Alas! Poor girl!" I commiserated. "How altered the world must appear!"

"Yes—and no. I find the houses bleak, the costumes ugly, and the sky depressing; (what perverse notion induces you to live in such a climate!) I find life less intelligently pursued and the people, consequently, less joyous. Yet my greatest surprise has been to encounter, on all sides, the familiar things I have always known. Can it be that in eighteen centuries you have achieved nothing more! No new thing!—no better thing, at least! Those sights which I have observed in your streets, in your parks, in your homes: is that all, the whole of your discoveries? . . . How really sad, my friend!" And she settled herself pensively in a chair.

As for me, the effect of her words, no less than her beauty, was such that I was dumb with astonishment; seeing which, she explained,

[100]

with a gracious smile:

"Thou seest this robe? It was placed with me in the tomb. Examine it closely. In my day, one dressed in wool, in flax, and in silk. On returning to the e a r t h, after all these centuries, I thought to find these old stuffs lost even to memory. I imagined (forgive me) that after so long a time men would have discovered marvellous tissues like the sunlight or moonlight and more grateful to the touch than the skin of a virgin or of a fruit. But you—how do you clothe yourselves? in wool, in flax, and in silk. . . Oh, to be sure: you have evolved cotton, fit to clothe negroes who were embarrassing in their natural state, and thereby achieved, perhaps, a moral purpose. . . Thou likest cotton? . . . This stuff which creeps and falls apart. . . Ugh! Thou exultest in its discovery? Myself, I would not touch it with the tip of my finger. Have you produced a stuff for covering b e t t e r than wool? No. Finer than the woven flax? more luminous than silk? . . But answer thyself.

"In that far-off day, we dressed our feet with skins, of which were made s a n d a l s, coloured shoes, furred slippers, high boots. See: thine own bicycling shoes, fastened with a loop a little higher, are Phrygian in form. Observe mine: they are of olive morocco, gilded with little irons, like the binding of a book. Admire them—thou wilt find none so cunning in the shops of thy friends' tradesmen."

[101]

She continued, after a little pause:

"We fashioned jewelry with two precious metals: gold and silver. Can you show me a third? Necklaces we had, rings, bracelets, earrings, diadems and brooches. All these I have found, identical in workmanship, along the Paris streets. You know the pearl, the emerald, the diamond, the o p a l, the moonstone, the r u b y, the sapphire and all the tinted silicas which Arabia and India yield, today, as formerly. Have you, in eighteen centuries, created, by chance, one precious gem? But one, tell me of one, I pray thee! one stone which my eyes have not known long ago, one ring which has not adorned my finger, one new jewel, even mounted in gold like mine, since thou hast no finer metal to offer me, but bearing in its claws a new rarity?"

Her earnestness had become augmented, little by little, to a tone of reproach and disappointment. I appealed to her with a deprecatory gesture:

"I think, Callisto," I replied, "That thou attachest undue importance to the ornaments which women love and which have no other function than to activate, by their difficult choice and fastidious form, a futile and stagnant life. It is manifest today, after ten thousand years of fruitless efforts among all people, that a young girl will never know how to be more beautiful by the art of the dressmaker, the embroiderer and the goldsmith than at the instant when she shows herself all naked, as the gods made her. I question not that the Greeks knew this simple costume. . ."

"Better than thou and thy compatriots."

"Yet you invented it not! Do not be proud. I know that, in our days, it is travestied more painfully than in the time when thou wert born; but at the worst, of what importance is the difference? One cannot dress women: that is axiomatic. We cannot counteract it. If æsthetic truths could be demonstrated from theorems, M. Poincaire could already have proved mathematically that it is futile to exercise human imagination in an attempt to solve this problem: as certain an impossibility as the trisection of angles. For my part, I am not concerned about a failure which persists because it is eternal, and I am content to admire woman in her primitive purity (which, for her, never changes), with the antique emotion of those who once touched Helen."

She regarded me steadily, and now, inclining her head toward me with her characteristic gesture, inquired significantly:

"Thou art sure, presumptuous one, that woman has not changed?"

II

My agitation was such that I have no clear recollection of what she did immediately after saying these words: how she divested herself of her rings, her four bracelets, her necklace, her marvellous robes, and, almost in a single gesture, let fall the heavy masses of her dark hair. So dazzling was the transition that it remains in my memory like a dimly-glimpsed wonder.

Until that moment, my senses had not entirely accepted the vision as a reality. Apparitions long believed supernatural and therefore recognized as obedient to the laws of a profound but mysterious nature, sometimes present themselves clothed in a material form which is not questioned by any of our senses and which can mislead even a spirit which is incredulous or simply fortified a g a i n s t improbabilities.

For an hour, then, I had been asking myself whether I was not being tricked by some extravagant reader: some stranger, I thought, tasteless enough and daring enough to come at night to a bed-chamber to which she had certainly not been invited, attempting, no doubt, to mask the banality of her design by an elaborate dissimulation aided by a costume from the theatre. I had responded in a mood which

she herself had induced, with the tolerant in-
dulgence and reserve of a complaisant interlocutor who, through amusement or curiosity,
would not rend too hastily the tissue of a careful and interesting comedy.

But when I saw her nude I comprehended at
once that she had come to me from the remote past. . .

I remember very well that, at the moment I
realized this, I approached, if I did not achieve,
all the exaltation with which a religious instinct invariably inspires me. I held myself in
my chair to keep from falling on my knees,
and I gazed, my head forward, with a feeling
of sacrilege, as though so marvellous a being
should not be beheld by the same eyes which
had seen mortal women. I had never known
such agitation.

Callisto was superb. Her body was slender
and rounded, the torso high, the legs long. Her
fine joints were of a fragility which ravished
me, and even in the muscular thighs one divined
the delicate bones. Her skin was depilated, but
pure and without cosmetics; it shone as though
fresh from the b a t h, with a pale uniform
brown, almost black about the breasts, along
the edges of the eyelids and in the short line
of sex. I know not how to describe her beauty
which could never be developed in our climate
or in our age, for it was not born of any one
detail but only of harmony and perhaps of
clarity. Her superiority to the women of my

time I was obliged to acknowledge without any proof for my discernment, as a connoisseur selects the true from the false, sometimes without being able to demonstrate the exact point upon which he bases his conviction.

As though proudly displaying her charms for my approbation, she extended herself upon the couch.

"At least," she resumed, with a smile, "You could have perfected women. Yet, as thou seest, the races have deteriorated. Your doctors, who despise ours, have left your mistresses, to-day, less beautiful than my sisters. The earth where we lived has not been engulfed. The Orontes descends always from the midst of the cedar mountains. Smyrna survives. Sparta is dead but Athens has been resurrected. O, vain and feeble age, why hast thou replaced the Ionians with a mixture of Levantines, and why hast thou not devoted the same ardour to creating selections of women as to perfecting families of roses? Thou canst not. Thine effort is that of a child. Ours was that of gods."

I was scarcely in a mood to dispute with her, for such a terror possessed me as one feels on the borderland of sleep: a terror lest she leave me suddenly, like a fluid born of the light. I asked myself if my eyes only had the illusion of her corporeal presence: if, with the tip of my finger, I could touch the delicate skin of her thigh.

She divined my thought.

"Come," she said, laughing, "I am not a vision. Give me thy hand."

Arching her loins upon the couch, she passed my arm about her body which yielded itself voluptuously to the pressure. Then with a waywardness which would not be turned aside, she continued her arraignment:

"A thousand years before the time of my beauty, men and women united somewhat as goats did. Thou hast read Homer? Neither Argos nor Troy knew pleasures other than the animals knew. Even the kiss upon the lips was unknown to Briseis. Andromache's breasts were never offered to other lips than those of her little child. About Helen's thighs no hand ever opened and lightly raised the shiverings born of the human caress."

Callisto closed her eyes. . .

"And then, suddenly, in a day, the ancient Orient of my birth took from the gods, like a fire immortally young, the sole gift which distinguished them from the other inhabitants of the world: they discovered voluptuousness.

"O days of strength! O youth of the world! For the first time, man's and woman's lips, forgetting fruits, found themselves savoury. The great burning soul of Aphrodite inspired the bodies of lovers and, each new day, a new pleasure—a new one, thou understandest— descended from blue Olympia into the great groaning beds. There was an unfettered in- toxication; from Babylon to Mount Erix, all

[107]

the perfumes, all the silks, the flowers, the arts and the women, formed in the triumph which followed the discovery of pleasure. Young girls, freed at last from hereditary savagery, conscious of their senses and their desires, opened their nostrils to the rose and their charming bodies to the mouth. During the centuries, the treasure of sensuality was enriched. In my time, in Antioch and in Alexandria, the women augmented it still more. I myself, Callisto, the daughter of Lamia, it was I who discovered this. . ."

But I drew back. . .

She laughed.

"What! Thou art afraid! Well, then, it is thy turn: speak! During the nineteen hundred years of my slumber in the tomb, what unknown joy have you wrested from the gods? Not long ago I asked thee for a new jewel. Now I ask thee for a caress which I have not already known. Without doubt, after so long a time, many new joys have been invented. I await thine invitation to partake of them."

Secure in her ironic position, she waited with mock expectancy. I divined that, during her long nocturnal wandering about the city, she had searched vainly for some novelty to reward her eagerness for new knowledge. I felt that I, alas! could offer nothing to this futile quest.

"Be patient," I said simply. "Thou seest, we have begun by forgetting everything. Later, we will re-invent. This is the history of modern civilization, which came to the world a few years after thy death, following unexampled calamities great enough to be irreparable. First came the birth and strange fortune of a religion which, in its origin, had something of d i v i n e inspiration but which, distorted by Israelites too crude or too adroit, shattered the culture of thy race and rained ashes upon the ruins of Athens. Upon its heels thundered the Barbarians; when the deluge of J u d e a had rotted the wood of the vessel, the rats penetrated and scattered it in pieces. This endured until the new day when those books rescued from destruction and recovered at Constantinople arose in the Orient like a new dawn. An hundred years were spent reading them. Since they have been studied, hardly three centuries have passed. But this age is for us, perhaps. We must be for the age, Callisto."

Her smile was derisive.

"Have you discovered," she responded, "in the parchments of your museums, the tradition of Rhodopis? Can your archaeologists, who know so thoroughly the policies of Pericles and the strategy of Alexander, reconstruct the science of Aspasia and of Thais? Are they sure that the tomb in which the delicate ashes of Phryne repose, has not enclosed forever the secret of a lost voluptuousness?

"I have it still, this tradition. Thou wouldst know it, perhaps? Come, I will disclose it to thee. . ."

[109]

III

While not unmindful of the curiosity of the young girls who may read this fragment of memories, I do not purpose to delay here and describe the events of that night: first, because I have already built, upon the materials furnished me by Callisto, a complete novel which I have called "Aphrodite"; second, because I feel myself restrained by a certain lingering reticence from delineating, under a personal form, the mysteries of a night of excesses.

Toward noon Callisto arose: pleasantly drawing me to observe that the sun was already high and that, through need of a perfected lighting system, we had scarcely seen one another.

"You destroy the Night: you no longer know the Dawn", she remarked, sadly. "Formerly, the spectacle of the light of dawn was the recompense for long exhausting vigils. Now you pass your lives in a monotonous light and you no longer know the Shadows."

I grew uneasy.

"Noon! . . . But thou didst tell me of a life restricted to the nocturnal hours. How can I still hold thee here?"

"That is an affair between Persephone and myself," she replied, with a strange smile. "Let us talk. I have not finished abusing thine epoch."

I was a little tired and still nervous.

"Enough, I pray thee! Let us talk of ourselves, rather; wilt thou? Let us leave the world, better or worse. . . I would hear only of thee."

"Still, hear me. I have not yet convinced thee. I will continue until I have done so. Truly, my second trip upon earth has saddened me. In the tomb, where I should have remained, I had my dreams of that purer age in which I grew up amidst pleasures. I yearn to tell someone about the deceptions which end my promenade, and what I wish to thy century for all the surprises which it has not offered me. Thou seest, the world is a young man who gives hopes, but who is likely to misfire his life."

"Yet I do not know. . . It seems to me that we have thought well and created well since thy death. The age in which we live is not so contemptible."

"But yes, it is! Partly from its impotence but more from its conceit. No: you have not thought and you have not created! You are like the Phoenicians, cunning in aping the models invented by my race, but elsewhere than with us you find nothing, and you exist only in our shadow."

Her gesture was one of sweeping scorn:

"Look around you in the Paris streets.

Everywhere our eternal soul shines in the facades of the monuments, in the capitals of the columns and on the foreheads of the statues. Now that the barbarous and sordid buildings erected during the middle ages are already (happily!) crumbling, you, men of these times, incapable of originality, have turned back to our ruins, and for four hundred years have made mosaics of stone with the fragments of our temples. A column found in Sicily has engendered two thousand c h u r c h e s and as many railroad platforms. You could not even give to new needs a new architecture! In the bronze of your cannons you have copied the Trajan column, and in your concert halls you have c a r r i e d on the Corinthian tradition. After us, with our sculptors who wrought in marble and cast in bronze, you have discovered nothing, not a natural stone, not a chemical alloy, worthy of reproducing the human form. And the only glory of your sculptors is not derived from what they have done, but that one of them has found, buried in the earth, a torso of Apollonius, a ruin without head, without arms and without legs, a lamentable wreck, but a created work, that: a created work. Thinkers!"

She took two books from a case and flung them upon the floor.

"Your thought, like your art, is a parasite upon our cadavers. It is not Descartes, it was Parmenides who said that thought is identical with being. It is not Kant, it was still Parmenides who said that thought is identical with its object. On these two precepts, the modern schools rest: they cannot break free. Wherever our science became general, that is to say philosophical, there it has remained, to this day, upon our fundamental laws. The masters of E u c l i d determined for all time the unchangeable relation of lines. Archimedes supplied integral calculus long before your Leibniz, who was equally indebted to us for his metaphysics. Instead of marvelling upon the fall of apples, your Newton, venerated one, might have limited himself to reading a page from Aristotle where his theory of universal gravity was expounded two thousand years ago. Upon the constitution of matter, which is the problem of God, Democritus knew more than Lord Kelvin; his hypothesis alone remains admissable. Finally, at the moment when you are upon the point of conceiving a central and universal science, with a law sufficient to explain all phenomena—what is this science and what is this law? No other than that to which Heraclitus, two thousand four hundred years ago, gave this definitive expression: fire transforms itself in movement, movement transforms itself in fire; and that is the world."

Exhausted, I threw my hands out, supplicatingly:

"O Callisto! Hear my weary words: thou art much too profound. I had often heard that antique courtesans were women of gifted minds, but it was not this, certainly, that constituted their charm. Today, if Madame de Pougy, in spite of her great literary talent, wished to entertain M. Boutroux with the subjects which preoccupy him, she would not succeed in interesting him as much as an Aspasia conversing with Xenophon. And yet I would prefer to have her tell me about a robe from Jacques Doucet than about a thermodynamic law, and it is a subject which would become her supple body. Moreover, the charm of a woman always increases at the moment when she is silent; but this subtle truth is perceptible only to men."

She waited patiently until I had finished: then, with victorious obstinacy, she charged afresh:

"How is it that, in two thousand years, you have discovered neither. . ."

"We discovered America," I interrupted her, impatiently.

"That is not true!"

"Do not be absurd, Callisto."

"I reiterate that it is not true! America was discovered by Aristotle, and this is not a paradoxical thesis but an historical and demonstrable fact. Aristotle knew that the world is round and (as thou canst learn from his books), he recommended a search for the road to the Indes 'by the west, beyond the columns of Heracles.' This is the project that Columbus resumed! Is not the glory of a discovery granted to the brain which conceives it, rather than to the one which executes it? When Leverrier discovered Neptune. . ."

"At least," I said, overcome with lassitude, "thou wilt concede that we discovered Neptune."

"So? And when was that! Discovered Neptune! I am astonished. Since yesterday I have been pleading with thee to reveal a new pleasure, a conquest toward happiness, a victory over tears. Neptune has been discovered! I return to this earth, after twenty centuries, concerned about all things, jealous of the marvels I supposed invented, beseeching, if I were not to weep through my life of eternal shadow, to be returned quickly to the world; and someone has discovered Neptune! A pleasure! a pleasure! a solace for the spirit or for the senses, it matters not which! Must I descend again to the Elysian fields without bearing with me the quiver of a new pleasure?"

Abruptly, then, she extended her olive hands:

"Anyway, it was Pythagoras who discovered Neptune."

I subsided.

"Unquestionably," she continued, relentlessly. "Pythagoras found that the solar system was composed of ten stars. I know not upon what he based this number: but his disciple, Philolaos, came to discern, later, without any lensed instrument, and many centuries before

Copernicus, the double movement of the earth upon its axis and about the central fire; although no doubt it is impossible for thee really to grasp how such a discovery could have been established with the sole equipment of reason, thou hast no right to assume that the hypothesis of Pythagoras was advanced rashly and confirmed by accident. There, I have finished!"

I contended no more.

"Wilt thou have a cigarette?" I asked.

"What?"

"I said: wilt thou have a cigarette? I doubt not they also are a heritage from the Greeks. It was Aristotle, perhaps, who. . ."

"No. I had never seen them before. We were ignorant, I admit, of this absurd habit of filling the mouth with the smoke of leaves. But surely thou dost not pretend to offer me this as a pleasure?"

"Who knows? Thou hast tried it?"

"Assuredly not! Thou, also, art a devotee of this droll practice?"

"Sixty times each day; it constitutes, in fact, the sole regular occupation in which my life is cheerfully employed."

"And it gives thee pleasure?"

"Surpassing the love of woman. I really believe I could refrain from woman's company for an entire week with greater fortitude than I could summon if deprived of my cigarettes for the same period."

"Surely thou art jesting."

[116]

"I was never more serious."

She had become thoughtful.

"Ah, well, then, do hand me a cigarette!"

"I suggest it."

"Wilt thou light it? And tell me, what is the custom? Does one simply breathe in and out?"

"Young girls merely puff the smoke; but that is insipid and superficial. One should inhale deeply. Draw in—so! Again. . . Close the eyes."

After a few tense moments, Callisto's little roll of oriental leaves was an ashy debris. Then she dropped the half-consumed end where the fard of her lips had left a circlet of rouge.

Silence.

She would not meet my eyes. She had taken, in a hand which trembled as if with some soft emotion, the little square package; and this, after I had seen her examine it on all sides, I knew that she would not relinquish.

Slowly, and with the care one bestows upon priceless objects, she placed it beside the ashtray at the end of a bright divan on which she disposed her long, dark body.

A NIGHT IN SPRING

I

Behind the garden-gate, Nephelis sat waiting, wrapped in a light cloak.

The darkness under the trees was so dense that their fragrance alone betrayed their silent presence. Nephelis could not see her hand before her eyes. All nature, human and inanimate, was asleep. The silence that brooded over the earth was as pure as the blackness of the shadows. Nephelis sat, motionless as a statue, her hands resting in her lap, her head slightly inclined toward one side.

Nor had she any desire to stir. Inexperienced, as became a wife, in the arts of seduction, she did not allow a fold of her wrap to flutter, lest the perfumes of her body be dispersed in the slumbering air. And, well knowing that she was in advance of the trysting time, she waited languidly, filled with a vision, intoxicated with hope.

Gently, a finger tapped the outside of the door.

Already! She noiselessly lifted the heavy bar, and the door swung on its oiled hinges.

She sensed a presence on the path, but she saw nothing except the impenetrable darkness.

"Follow me without speaking," she murmured. "I will precede thee; come quickly; I am afraid of the slaves, lest one of them see us. Follow me closely. There, beyond the thickets, thou wilt be able to see my shadow."

She walked on tip-toe, her little s a n d a l s barely touching the sand or the mosaic pavement. As she grazed a branch, she shuddered. A furtive rustling pervaded the vast stillness, and the stirring flowers threw out their perfume.

The first to enter her c h a m b e r, she ran eagerly to a niche where she had so placed a screen as to shade, without obliterating, an earthen lamp. She turned up the light, then faced her companion.

"O Gods!" she cried, "Great Gods! It is not he!"

The man had advanced to the centre of the floor. She retreated toward the wall until her back struck it heavily, and her hands wandered tremblingly over its surface.

"Who art thou?"

"I am not *he*, as thou hast said. Art thou quite sure of that? There is a *he*, is there not, and the rest of the world? I, I am the rest, humanity, the c r o w d, of which nothing is wanted."

Terrified, Nephelis stared at him. He was

an angular man, with a heavy beard which accented his leanness. His head seemed composed entirely of hair. Four teeth were missing from his upper jaw, so that his moustache fell mingling with his beard, and this detail was horrible. His bony neck protruded from a woollen cloak which was fantastically draped and very dirty. His legs appeared shorter than his body He was neither large nor small, but the lamp, set on the ground, magnified his body in a towering shadow, spreading over the wall and half of the ceiling.

Violently he crossed his arms and thrust his hands under his arm-pits.

"Aha!" he exclaimed. "The scented couch! rose leaves! an amphora of rich wine! Someone was expected, that favoured *he* who is not me. When the husband makes war, the wife makes mischief. Ha! Ha! Coronals of flowers! . . But I smell myrrh, which sickens me. . . And this lamp with its black smoke. . . That smells of prostitution in thy house, dost thou hear me? . . . Hello! Take off thy robe and ply thy trade! Here is a drachma."

A piece of silver went spinning through the air and struck Nephelis in the belly. She stifled a scream.

"Wretched man!" she said, in a thin voice, "Thou shalt know what it will cost thee to speak thus to me. Yes, I have a husband, and I have a lover, but the door of the garden has opened again; *he* is there, in the passage; he

[123]

is coming; he approaches; and if he finds thee here he will kill thee like a worm."

"Kill me!" echoed the unknown. "And how will he kill me? I have been dead these hundreds of years. Thou askest my name? I am the king of Egypt, embalmed."

A thrill of fear swept through Nephelis' veins, and she passed her hand slowly over her mesmerized face.

"I am lost," she exclaimed, in despair. "He is mad."

Seeing her pallor, the man resumed, smiling:

"Do not cry out, my lovely one, or I will kill thee; and for thee, who hast not yet tasted death, this will mean more than it would to a corpse like me. See my mummied flesh."

With a sudden gesture, he cast aside his vestments and stood before her nude.

"Thou didst lie when thou said just now that the gate had opened again; for that is impossible. The bar is in place. There is no one in the garden, nor in the passage. Get to thy business, my girl, I have given thee thy pay. And do not make a noise or, by Zeus, I will slay thee quickly."

Nephelis would, at that moment, have welcomed death. Her fright far surpassed that which the dead feel at the sight of the eternal Lethe. . . But death by this man— Oh! what could be more terrible!

She did not cry out.

With a supreme effort, knowing that the

insane should not be contradicted, she jerked out a few phrases, painfully articulated by her dry, cold tongue:

"Yes, thou art King of Egypt. . . thou art covered with little bands. . . But it is beneath thy dignity, Lord, to remain in the house of thy servant. . . Shall I show thee the path? . . . Thy queens, fairer than all women, sing at the gates of the garden."

The madman started.

"King! King! Nonsense! Who said I was a king? Do I look like a man? Is it not evident that I am a god? How could I have entered here, benighted fool, if I had not been a god? The door is barred: I told thee, the bar is in its sockets. I did not enter by the door. I am the emanation of that black amphora. I am Bacchus! Bacchus!"

Clamping the coronal of roses on his head, he began to dance wildly about the room.

Imperceptibly, Nephelis slipped along the wall, seeking to reach a place from which she could take flight. The madman, whirling around in the delirium of his bacchanal, did not observe her; but, as she stooped toward the lock, she felt a bony hand drop upon her shoulder. It was the first time he had touched her. She recoiled once more to the depths of the chamber.

"Ah!" he breathed, pausing, "Thy skin is fresh, my girl. Why dost thou not disrobe? Remove that covering! I have paid thee."

He approached her and tore the loose, thin garment away from one of her breasts. Nephelis flattened herself against the wall. She tried to speak, but not a word came from her quivering lips. . . The madman's fingers grasped the shapely b r e a s t, pressing it between his fingers: a thin jet of milk spirted out.

At this sight he paled, and his voice changed; it became like that of a little child.

"Mama," he cried, "Mama! Why hast thou not nursed me, these hundreds of years? What have I done that thou shouldst give thy breast to another, to him whom thou awaitest in a bed of roses and perfumes? Is it because I no longer have teeth, that thou wilt not nurse me? Mama! Why hast thou abandoned me?"

And, grasping the despairing Nephelis' arms with his two hands, he ardently set his lips to the n i p p l e and sucked it thirstily. A start of horror gave fresh strength to the young woman.

"Monster!" she cried. "It is my child's milk thou drinkest!"

She shook herself free and grasped the man by his hairy throat. But in an instant he had subdued her.

"Ha! Ha!" he cried. "I told thee no one could kill a corpse! On the other hand, it is easy, as thou shalt see, to slay a living woman. . . Ha! Ha! No! Do not shriek. I will not slay thee. This is a game; a festival. Give me thy hair-ribbon."

[126]

Seizing the band from her long hair, which fell silently, he secured from behind her two wrists and bound them tightly upon her loins.

Her teeth chattering, she tried to cry out, but a last hope sustained her. . . The garden door had *not* been closed. . . *He* was coming, her lover, her saviour; *he* would deliver her. . . Ah! how she yearned for him! In what a frenzied burst, all the energy of her desire strained toward him!

The madman, meanwhile, had removed her girdle and detached the clasp and silver buckle on her right shoulder. Her vestment sank to the floor. In vain she closed her knees. The man snatched away the robe and, grasping the unfortunate girl about the waist, threw her upon the bed where she fell, moaning.

The odour of perfumes mounted from the shaken couch.

"Ah! That smell of myrrh!" the madman cried again. "Thy kennel is infected, daughter of joy! Ha! Out with the myrrh! Down with it! Down with it! . . . I am Psammetichus, son of the Sun. Myrrh is the essence of the Night. I am the vanquishing King, the Highest, the King! the King! Myrrh is the stench of filthy caverns. Out with the myrrh, daughter of the Night! By the horns of Hathor and by the jaws of Pasht! Down with it! Down with it! Down with it!"

He subsided at last, his head bent.

Nephelis, cowering at the extremity of the couch, watched him, wide-eyed.

A great calm fell. The man was silent. Outside, the same nocturnal hush hovered over the deserted garden. Then *he* was not coming! Gods! Perhaps *he* had come, *he* had knocked, *he* had not entered the door, *he* had gone . . . gone. . . A cruel anguish locked her throat.

And the madman recovered himself.

"Ah, thou art lovely!" he said, in a soft voice. "How long hast thou been my wife? Thou wert not like this when I was king. Thy blonde hair has become black. Thy narrow flanks have become larger. . . And thy legs! . . Oh, thy legs are very ample. . . Open them. . ."

He went on murmuring to her, resting his hand on a marble tabouret which held vials of perfumes.

"Fear not," he said. "I am old. Thou seest, my girl, that I am an old man. . . I have been dead an hundred years. Do not turn away from a mummy. I d e s i r e only to kiss thy mouth, and to sleep, to sleep upon thy breast, oh mother."

His bony hands advanced slowly, as though in supplication. But he was stopped by a nervous spasm that shook him from head to foot. He leaped upon the bed, over the girl, and fell on the other side.

"Aaaah!"

She had cried out at last! A long cry like a wail, a rending of her whole soul, a despairing plaint for rescue, to the gods, for a miracle, for life!

"Help! Help!" screamed the m a d m a n. "Cease struggling, daughter of the N i g h t! Close not thy small teeth, my kiss shall penetrate thee! Ha! the myrrh! the myrrh! Thou shalt conceive, be sure. Stars issue from thy breast like bees from a hive! Ha! ha! ha! For I am old. . . old. . ."

Nephelis had freed her right hand and, with a movement so deft that the madman saw it not, she seized a solid object from the tabouret and struck him on the temple. She drew herself upright on the couch, her mouth open, her hands before her face, and a sort of laughter shook her that was more frightful than any moaning. The man had fallen under the blow, but he was not dead. She drew quickly from a slender vase her long hair-pins, ten or twelve sharp points of which any one would be fatal, and, twenty times and more, she plunged them all into his lean hairy chest, between his projecting ribs, into his stomach, abdomen, eyes and cheeks.

The slaves, awakened by her cries, hurried in to find her trampling upon the c o r p s e, smeared with blood, entirely naked and with her hands uplifted toward the sky, like an impossible Andromeda who had triumphed over the Beast.

THE ARTIST VICTORIOUS

I

We stood in the green gardens of white Ephesus, two young disciples, before the aged sculptor, Bryaxis. The seat upon which he sat was as pallid as his face. He did not speak nor look up, but lightly struck the earth again and again with the end of his staff.

We remained there patiently, out of deference for his great age and his greater glory. Leaning against two dark cypress trees, we were silent, eagerly waiting to hear him speak. He appeared to be unconscious of the mute homage in our attitude. It was wonderful to reflect that he had survived all those great beings whom we had longed to know. We loved to have him reveal his spirit to us, for we were simple-hearted youths, born too late to have heard the voices of heroes. We sought to trace the almost invisible bonds that united him to his amazing life-work. We mused to ourselves that the brow before us had conceived, that hand had helped to model, a frieze and twelve figures for the tomb of Mausolus, the King of Caria, a work that was a wonder of the world: the five Colossi erected in front of the town of Rhodes, the Bull of Pasiphæ, that made women dream strange dreams, the formidable Apollo of bronze, and the Seleucus Triumphant.

The more I contemplated the creator of these wonder-works, the more it seemed to me that the gods must have fashioned him with their own hands, that he might be the means of revealing them to the hearts of men!

We were aroused suddenly by a rush of feet, a whistle, and a gay light-hearted cry; the young Ophelion stood before us.

"Bryaxis," he cried, "hear now what all the city knows. Artemis shall receive my thank-offering if I should perchance be the first to tell thee. But first let us make our salute: I had forgotten."

He now turned towards us, as if to say, "Prepare yourselves well for what I am about to tell you." Then he continued thus:

"Revered one, you have heard that Clesides painted the Queen's portrait?"

"People have spoken about it to me."

"But have they told you the end of the story?"

"I was not aware that there was a story connected with it."

"A story! . . Listen, for you are ignorant of all! Clesides came by appointment from his native Athens. He was escorted to the Palace. The Queen permitted herself to be late, and did not appear for some time. When at last she presented herself, she scarcely took cognizance of her artist, but threw herself at once into what one, by courtesy, may call a pose. For she continually moved and shifted her attitude, under the pretext that Love had given her a cramp. Clesides drew in a very bad humour, as you may suppose. He had not even finished his rough sketch, when lo! the Queen announced that she would now pose for her back. . .!"

"Without a reason?"

"The reason she gave was that her back was as admirable as the rest of her body, and must appear in the picture. In vain did Clesides protest that he was a painter and not a sculptor, that one does not turn a picture to see its back; that one cannot represent a woman from every side upon the one flat plane of a canvas. . . To all these objections, the Queen responded, unmoved, that it was her will; that the laws of art were not her laws; that she had seen the portrait of her sister as Persephone, of her mother as Demeter; and that she, Queen

Stratonice, by her sole self, wished to be drawn in the character of the 'Three Graces'."

"It was not, after all, such a stupid idea of hers," said Bryaxis.

The narrator appeared to be indignant at this remark.

"Supposing that Clesides had replied, 'No'? He was free to do so, one would think. Artists are not accustomed to taking orders. Such a thing as that we could *not* support. Never would the Queen's father, Demetrius, have countenanced such a thing. Why, when he laid siege to Rhodes, where at the time Protogenes resided, Demetrius refused to fire that part where the sculptor worked."

"I am familiar with that story. Proceed," said Bryaxis.

"Very well; I will be brief. Clesides was very angry, but concealed his feeling. He finished his study of the back, and the Queen rose, asking him to return on the morrow; he agreed, and took his leave. Very good. On the morrow what awaited him? A servant, bringing the message that the Queen Stratonice was fatigued, and would not pose any more. The servant was to pose for her until the portrait was finished. *That* was what the Queen had desired!"

We were convulsed with merriment, in which Bryaxis joined us.

Ophelion continued gaily:

"The slave was not badly formed. Clesides

gave her the same opportunity to be cramped
that her mistress had, and then told her in a dry
way that he did not need her any more. There-
upon he gathered up his drawings, and left."

"And he was justified," I said. "The Queen
was making sport of him."

"Well, on the way home, as he passed near
the port, he caught sight of a mariner who
was reported—though without convincing
proof—to have been the Queen's lover; his
name was Glaucon, whom you know by sight.
Clesides persuaded the fellow to come home
with him, and sit for four days. At the end
of that time, he had produced two scandal-
ous little drawings, representing the Queen
in the arms of the sailor, first facing the be-
holder, and then with the back showing. These
pictures he took out one night and fastened to
the wall of the Palace of Seleucus. He then
disappeared, after this public retaliation, and
no trace of him was found thereafter. The
Queen knows of it already, and if she is furious at heart, she hides it marvellously.

"All that morning an interminable crowd
defiled before these outrageous paintings.
Stratonice, being told of it, desired to see them
herself. Accompanied by twenty-five people
of her court, she stopped before the two
subjects, approaching and then retreating as
though the better to judge of their artistic or
truthful aspect in detail and in general. I was
present, and as I followed her movements with

a feeling of apprehension, wondering on whom she would fasten her vengeance when her anger reached its peak, I heard her say:

"I cannot decide which is the better; both are excellent!"

In the midst of our exultation, Bryaxis lifted his eyebrows, and so gave to his face the fine old lines that denoted surprise.

"She proved that she is not less witty than impudent," he commented. "The whole episode is very curious; but why do you betray such pride or such pleasure in the conduct of its hero? Is not the part played by the model a very important one?"

"Had the Queen been brave," said Ophelion, "she would have pursued Clesides even to the far-off seas, and there sentenced him to be killed as if he were a dog. But then, through all the violet land of Greece, she would have been considered none other than a barbarian woman—she who would fain be accepted as a thorough Athenian! Stratonice holds Asia in her hand as though it were a fly, and she has drawn back before a man who has for his weapons only a tablet and stylus. . . Hereafter the Artist is the king of kings, the sole inviolable being living under the sun. Now you understand why we are proud!"

The old man's nostrils dilated in disdain.

"Thou art young," he replied. "In my own youth we said the same thing, and perhaps with greater reason. When Alexander timidly tried to point out why such and such a picture struck him as very fine, my friend Apelles silenced him by saying that he was giving amusement to the boys who ground up the colours; and Alexander apologized. Ah, well! I do not believe that such tales really repay one for the trouble of telling them. Whatever may be the attitude—the respect or arrogance —of the King towards contemporary painters, their work is not any the better, or any the worse, for it; the effect upon art, either way, is negligible. On the other hand, it may be good, and even noble, for an artist to dare and to be able to put himself, not above the King marching with an army near the walls of his home, but above all human laws, or even divine laws, when the Muses, his governing forces, dictate his course."

Bryaxis had risen. We murmured in wonder:

"But who has done that? Of whom do you speak?"

"No one, perhaps," was the abstracted answer of the old artist, and there came into his eyes the far-off look of the dreamer, "unless the great Parrhasius. . . Did he act wisely, I wonder? I used to believe so, but today I doubt, and know not what to think."

Ophelion threw me an astonished look, but I could not enlighten him as to the meaning underlying Bryaxis' words.

"We do not follow you, Bryaxis," he said.

[139]

He answered, as if to hint at his meaning:
"The Prometheus of Parrhasius."

"Yes; but what is the story?"

"Do you not know how Parrhasius painted the Prometheus of the Acropolis?"

"No. We have never been told."

"You do not know of that terrible scene—the deathly tragedy and alarums from whence that picture emerged, blood-stained?"

"Speak! Tell us all the scene, and how it came about. We do not know."

For an instant, the aged artist rested his eyes upon our young faces, as if he hesitated to burden our spirits with such a revelation. Then he said resolutely:

"Very well. You shall hear about it."

II

The events which I am about to relate to you fell in the year of Plato's death. I was in Halicarnassus at that time, engaged upon my part of the labour that was to produce at last the great tomb of King Mausolus the Long-haired. It was a thankless task, if the truth were known. Scopas, who directed all of us, had decided to decorate the whole of the eastern front of the monument himself, so that in the early sunlight, when the people sacrificed, the marbles of our master were resplendent in the full glow, and, truly, they saw little of the other work.

To his comrade of the chisel, Timotheus, he had given the lateral face of the monument, south; less interesting and more extended. Leochares was entrusted with the western front. As for me, I had taken that side others had not wanted—the northern, an enormous piece of work which lay perpetually in shadow.

(Pithis was also employed in raising a pyramid over this stately monument, and the top was adorned by a chariot harnessed to four horses. The expenses of this edifice were terrific, and this fact inspired the philosopher Anaxagoras to exclaim when he saw it: "How much money changed into stones!")

Over a period of five years, I sculptured

[141]

Victories and Amazons that appeared, in the sun, like living women; but each time it became necessary for me to fix one forever in the shadow of the monument, it seemed to me that the look of life died out of the stone form, and my grief drew tears from my eyes. At last my task came to an end. I occupied myself with preparations for returning into Attica. In that year, as today, the Ægean Sea was treacherous: war raged everywhere, and strife arose daily between the cities. Besides, Athens was vanquished. The day upon which I planned to take my departure, I could not find a ship-master, or owner of a privateer, who was willing to go to the Piræus. The people of Caria, good traders, turned towards the vanquisher, and from the time that the taking of Olynthus had let Chalcis fall into the hands of the Macedonians, all the merchants of Halicarnassus filled out t h e i r sails for Eubœa, where Venus was worshipped as the principal deity, in order to sell silken robes of Cos to the courtesans of Cnidus.

I, also, departed for Chalcis. The voyage by sea was almost intolerable to me. I was not treated well, even in the little corner of the vessel with which I affected to be satisfied. My name in those days had not the same sound and report as it has today, and the great monument to Mausolus was too recent and too familiar to men's minds. The other voyagers upon the ship knew me merely as a citizen of

Athens. That quite sufficed to incite their irony, for Athens was then an unfortunate city.

One morning, when the sun was high, we landed at Chalcis in the midst of an immense crowd in which I lost myself, and with pleasure. A question elicited the information that there was, outside the gates, an extraordinary market. Philip, at the fall of Olynthus, after having pillaged the city, had reduced to slavery the whole of the population.

The captives numbered about forty-five thousand. The slave-market, which had been created to dispose of these unfortunate persons, had been in action for two days, and might continue for three months. The city was also thronged with strangers—purchasers and curiosity-seekers. My interlocutor, who was a dealer in wines, did not complain, but he confided to me that his neighbour, whose business had been to sell costly slaves, was ruined. I heard a tavern-keeper say with many gestures: "Consider, a Thracian of twenty years of age, one knows what he is worth, by all the Gods. When one has bought twelve to cultivate land, one counts twelve bags of gold. Now mark the price, it has fallen to fifty drachmas. Judge of the others by that only. Such a thing has never been heard of. There are three thousand virgins up for sale. They will go for twenty-five drachmas apiece, and please do not imagine that I speak extravagantly. Perhaps those with the whitest skins may fetch a few drachmas more. Ah! Philip is a great king indeed!"

Wearied of his chattering, I left him, and followed the multitude beyond the open gates of the city to the vast stretch of country where the Olynthians were camped. With infinite pains I forced my way through the many groups in movement. Suddenly I saw pass near me a procession of luxurious and majestic aspect. The crowds fell away to the left and right.

First advanced six Sarmatian slaves, armed, and marching in pairs. Behind them a little Ethiopian held horizontally a long cross of cedar decorated with gold. It was the stick of the Master. Finally, gigantic and heavy, crowned with flowers, the beard impregnated with perfumes, and his body draped in a capacious purple robe, Parrhasius himself came into view. He walked as though he scorned the submissive earth beneath his feet. Each arm encircled the shoulders of a beautiful maiden. He looked, for all the world, like the Indian Bacchus.

He called out, as his eyes fell upon me:

"If you are not Bryaxis, who gave you permission to bear his face?"

"And you," I replied, "if you are not the son of Semele, who has given you that Dionysiac stature and that robe of purple, woven by the Graces of Naxos?"

He smiled upon me, and without removing

his great arms from their lovely resting-places, he seized and shook my hand, pressing it against the bared breast of one of his companions.

"Chariclo," (to the young girl upon his right), "take an arm of my friend, and let us resume our promenade. Soon the sun will wax too fierce to be pleasant."

As he desired, we walked along amorously enlaced. Parrhasius strode with a grand heavy balancing of the body, like the pompous measure of a hexametre, while the little steps of the women were as a dactyl. In a few words, he drew from me an account of my works and my life. At each of my responses, he said vividly, "Yes. I understand perfectly." He wished to cut short any prolonged speech. Then he began to speak of himself.

"Understand at once," he said, "that I have taken you under my protection. For not one citizen of Athens, save myself alone, is out of danger when near the Macedonian. If any tiny disturbance had brought you before their Court of Justice, I would not have given two copper coins for the value of your liberty. But now, you may be of an easy mind."

"Though not of a timorous turn," I answered, "yet here, in the shadow of your mighty name—"

"Yes," said Parrhasius. "When Philip knew that I was going to honour his new city he sent forward upon my route an officer of the palace. This person brought me royal gifts,

[145]

among others the six colossal men slaves and the two beautiful girls that you have seen. That is to say, Force to spread wide my path, and Beauty to enchant my leisure."

"Girls of Macedonia?" I inquired.

"Macedonians of Rhodes," came the laughing answer.

And then, with a magnanimous gesture of his arm, Parrhasius said:

"Take them. They shall both brighten your bed this night. As for me, I have others left with my valuables. But you are alone, my friend. Accept these rosy flowers of flesh from my hands. Their young vivid skins will be charming in contrast with a couch of deep purple. . ."

We had reached the great market. He stopped and regarded me.

"Why is it that you do not ask me on what mission I came?"

"I would not dare."

"Can you divine it?"

"I cannot. You do not want slaves, for Philip gives you his own. Nor girls, since, as you say. . ."

"I have come from Athens to Chalcis to find a model, my friend. Now you seem astonished."

"A model. . . for you! Are there not any, then, between the Academe and the Piræus?"

"About half a million—for me," he replied, grandly. "All Athens, it is true. Yet I seek a

model at the sale of the Olynthians. You shall hear why, and you will grasp my purpose."

Here he drew himself up proudly.

"I shall make a Prometheus."

His face reflected the horror that the mention of Prometheus naturally evokes.

"Every portico," he continued, "has a Prometheus, of one sort or the other. Timagoras made and sold one; Apollodorus has attempted another. Zeuxis, too, believed that he had the power . . . but why recall to our minds the memory of so much futile daubing? *The* Prometheus has yet to be given to the world."

"That I fully believe," I answered him.

"These pygmies have fashioned peasants naked and attached to rocks made of wood; their faces distorted by a grimace of some sort, as if they had a tooth-ache. But, Prometheus, the forger of fire, the creator of the man and his struggle with the eagle-god. . . Ah! No one has yet realized that, Bryaxis. Such a Prometheus, one of the utmost grandeur, conceived by my brain, executed by my hands, haunts me; I see it as clearly as I see your face. That is the great Prometheus that will one day be placed on the walls of the Parthenon."

So saying, he quitted the support of his girl companion, took his wand of wood and gold, and traced great waves of outline in the air.

"Upon my great scheme I have worked for two months. I have found splendid rocks in the domain of Crates, at the Promontory of

[147]

Astypolus. All these studies were finished, the foundation of my picture ready, the line of the figure in its place. All at once, I am stopped at white heat. I fail to find a head. If it was merely a question of a Hermes, an Apollo, or a Pan, any citizen of Athens would be proud to pose before me. But to take for model a man whose face is shining with genius, and to tie, or bind, him by the ankles, the hands, no, you can see for yourself that it is impossible. One cannot dislocate the limbs of one of these as one would the limbs of a slave. We lack slaves who have the heads of freeborn Greeks. Ah, well, Philip brings us some like that, and I come to buy where Philip comes to sell."

I could not forbear a shudder.

"An Olynthian!" I said, "one of the vanquished. But where do you intend to finish this masterpiece?"

"At Athens."

"Upon the soil of Athens your slave will be free."

"When I wish it; not before."

"But have you no fear whatever of the laws that will protect your captive?"

"The laws?" Parrhasius smiled. "I hold the laws in the hollow of my hand, even as the folds of this mantle that I now throw over my shoulder."

And with a royal gesture he seemed to envelop himself, at one time, with the rich purple and the glorious sunshine.

III

The Olynthian slave-market now loomed before us. As far as the eye could reach, platforms of planks, erected upon tressels at a height of about a yard from the g r o u n d, formed a straight line in six parallel directions. The population of an entire city was there exposed before the population of another city: the one offered as merchandise to the o t h e r. Twenty-five t h o u s a n d men, women, and children, their hands bound behind the back, their ankles shackled with loose cords, waited, for the m o s t p a r t standing—waited for the unknown master who was yet to come, purchase, and lead them to some strange spot in the land of Greece. One soldier guarded forty of them; servants in crowds circulated with the bread and water needed for the sustenance of such a host of slaves. A great and murmurous noise perpetually ascended to the sky. It was like the uproar of a huge banquet.

Parrhasius penetrated before me into the principal "street" of slaves, where were exposed for sale young men and young girls who seemed qualified, for one reason or another, to command a price higher than the average. I felt some astonishment that their eyes did not express any great misery; they seemed merely curious. Then I reflected that human sadness,

[149]

for the young, has its certain measure, and even now these beautiful beings were anticipating the coming of their master, as a moderation of their pains. From the time of the destruction of their homes, they had experienced to the full all that could darken their days and nights with despair. The young men no doubt had regained hope of their future escape: the young women perhaps dreamed of a love that might promise them a little happiness. Whether induced by bravado or by sheer ignorance, their mood seemed to be one of patience and good humour. The crowd pressed around them, examining them in a state of indecision as to which ones to purchase. Few could have decided quickly where the choice was so wide. Often the slaves were handled, while prospective purchasers tested the muscles of a leg, the delicacy of a skin, the firmness of a breast. Then they were passed over in favour of a possible better bargain.

Parrhasius halted tentatively before a girl whose tall white figure was a symphony of graceful lines.

"Behold," he remarked, "this is a beautiful child."

A hawker at once came forward and burst into a voluble harangue:

"She is the loveliest one offered for sale, my lord. See how straight she is, and white. Sixteen years old yesterday."

"Eighteen years," corrected the girl.

"You lie, by Zeus! She is but sixteen years old, my lord; do not credit her when she says otherwise. Look at her black tresses held up by this comb. When she uncoils them, they fall to her knees. Examine her long white fingers, untouched by any labour. She is the daughter of a senator."

"Speak not of my father," said the girl, gravely.

"She is beautiful as a water-nymph, supple as a sword, and a virgin—as at her birth."

The fellow disrobed her with cynical hands, but Parrhasius struck the earth with his stick, muttering:

"A virgin, you say? What care I whether she be virgin or not, if only she be beautiful enough. Take away her shackles, that she may clothe herself properly. I will purchase her. What is her name?"

"Artemidora," said she.

"Very good. Then know, Artemidora, that you are now a part of the retinue of Parrhasius."

She opened wide her great eyes, hesitated charmingly, and then inquired:

"You are the Parrhasius who. . ."

"I am Parrhasius," he answered.

Then, consigning her to the care of his guard, he again walked on. Presently he deigned to explain to me:

"Bound to the Caucausus that young creature would be wonderful! Nevertheless, she will not be my Prometheus. I shall use her as a model for certain little erotic pictures with which I ease my toils during hours of leisure —pictures that are not, however, the least noble part of my life-work."

We walked on. The crowd had thickened. The sun became more intense in the midst of that vast plain, without a shadow, and the heat of that great and mixed concourse of people was almost infernal.

The girl Artemidora was arrayed in a white tunic, girdle, and veil. She often turned to look at us, and she seemed, when properly robed, to be a different person. Her face had acquired another expression, that of eagerness to glean from one of us the identity of the man to whom she was fated to surrender. Already we had traversed half the principal street, when the master stopped, and said:

"No. That for which I seek shall not be found here. The youth of the body and the beauty of the face are not found together. I have more chance, I think, of finding my man among slaves of the second class."

We had scarcely covered three more paces, when he threw out his hand, with an exultant gesture, and cried out:

"Behold the man!"

I drew near and gazed intently at the one to whom he pointed. He was a man of about fifty years of age, of a fine, tall figure, and excellent proportions. His face was large and

[152]

striking; the arch of the brows was powerful and muscular, the nose and ears were correctly modelled, the hair grey, but the beard brown and brindled. The strong muscles of the neck formed a noble pedestal for his head, and gave it an air of authority.

Parrhasius questioned him.

"What do you call yourself?"

"Outis."

"I do not ask you for anything, my brave man, but the name that you received from your father."

"For a month past I have called myself Outis. If I have ever borne another, older name, it does not please me to tell you."

"Why not?"

"It does not please me to tell you why, Son of a Dog!"

Parrhasius became purple with anger. The seller of the slaves, alarmed, advanced toward him with suppliant gestures.

"Do not attend to him, my lord. He speaks as one who has lost his senses, but that is pure malice on his part, for he has more brain-power than I have. He is a physician. For science and skill he has not his equal in all Olynthus. I say what all the world would repeat, for he was celebrated even in Macedon. I have been told that during thirty years he has cured more Olynthians than we were able to kill when we took their city. This will be a precious slave when he is chained, and has felt the rod. He plays the insolent, but he will change his tone, as all the others will do, or have done. Then, if you lead him away with you, Death will not come to you till your hundredth winter! Give me thirty drachmas, and this Nicostratus will be your chattel forever."

"Nicostratus," repeated Parrhasius to me. "I know a poet of that name; but my indifference towards the science of medicine is profound."

Turning towards the seller, he ordered him to remove the slave's clothes.

Nicostratus, helpless, yet disdainful, permitted this to be done. Parrhasius compelled him to assume first one position and then another for some time. At last the bargain was struck. Parrhasius did not conceal his joy. "Superb!" he pronounced.

I felt almost envious, and I did not reply.

It is fifty years—the space of a human life —since that episode. I have seen hundreds and hundreds of models, but never one worthy to be compared with that Nicostratus the Olynthian. He was the Image of Man in all his grandeur, at the full age of force and power. I never had him as a model for any work of mine; for the unhappy being posed only once, and you shall now learn how.

IV

I returned to my own country, going through Attica on horseback. During my absence of five years, creditors had seized and converted into gold the few poor goods that I possessed, and I lived very simply at a hostelry of Athens for many weeks. Parrhasius followed after an interval of a few days. Hearing of my modest lodging, he at once offered me hospitality. I went to his house, for the purpose of thanking him and declining his invitation. He then lived near the Academy, in a palace of marble and metal, close to the house that Plato occupied.

The gardens extended to the river, and the house was surrounded by much pomp of trees and shrubbery. By some strange mental quirk which is incongruous with his true greatness of soul, Parrhasius loved ostentation and indulged in every show of wealth. His fortune was immense, and he did not permit any one to think otherwise. Costly marble, silk, gold, and beauteous women gave his home the air of a palace of Artaxerxes. Standing, robed in scarlet silk, and crowned like an Olympian god, he received me upon the threshold of the chamber that served him for a studio. I then accompanied him into the famous salon that had been the matrix of so many masterpieces.

[155]

"My Prometheus?" he said, in answer to my first eager question. "No: I am yet meditating upon that. In a few days I shall see it all more clearly. Come; look at this trifle. Is it not charming? I have never done a more beautiful thing."

My eyes followed his gesture to a picture of a sleeping nymph and two satyrs. Near it, I saw the lovely Artemidora and two of the Sarmatians, from which it was not difficult to divine that they had been posing for the work.

He ordered them to resume their attitude, and then continued the painting before me.

V

For a whole month I remained at Athens, occupied with my own personal affairs; and these did not allow me time to return to the house of the great painter. Athens was truly in mourning since the fall of the Olynthians. The slave-market at Chalcis, the sale of a nation, such a scandal and outrage was the subject on all tongues, and the thought of all who were silent.

One day the report spread that in Athens a citizen held captive an Olynthian woman. The citizen was tried, condemned, executed.

Alarmed, I hastened to Parrhasius, at whose door my entreaties gained me admission. . . Never shall I forget the regard, slow and grave, with which Parrhasius greeted me at my entrance. He was standing, at work. Following his further glances, I saw, to my horror, the nude figure, bound to an actual rock, of Nicostratus the Olynthian.

"Cry out!" shouted Parrhasius to him; and his awesome captive did so, cursing, foaming, and raging.

The face of Parrhasius did not alter one line. He said to a Sarmatian slave: "Upon his right; touch lightly, without penetrating." Nicostratus watched the man advance, then his eyes swooned, and a sweat of agony broke out on

[157]

his temples. Moans issued from the lips; then a sob, like that of a child. Parrhasius, impassible, studied the face; then suddenly exclaimed: "Imbecile! He has died too soon."

* * * * * *

When the people of A t h e n s knew how Parrhasius had painted his Prometheus, they stormed his house, clamoring for death to the homicide. At last Parrhasius, in all his regal pomp and splendour, a p p e a r e d before the angry, threatening mob. Then, slowly, reverently, as though offering something sacrosanct, he lifted the curtain of his p a i n t i n g, and showed the Athenian people the Prometheus.

An awesome hush, and a shudder of utmost wonder and amazement, followed the superb revelation. It was not a painting they saw but a living portrayal of human anguish and final defeat by death. The summit of tragic grandeur seemed to be unveiled there for the first time in the world's history... Silence like that which reigns in a temple, held the people for the space of a few heart-beats; then some s c a t t e r e d hostile cries arose here and there. But they were futile, and died, lost in the overwhelming thunder of glory.

THE COLLECTED TALES

OF PIERRE LOUŸS

PART II

WOMAN AND PUPPET

I

Wherein it is seen that one word on an eggshell may establish a perfect understanding.

In Spain the Carnival does not close, as in France, at eight o'clock on Ash Wednesday morning. The colourful gaiety of Seville is subdued for only four days by the sombre hovering memory that "Dust we are, etc."; and the first Sunday in Lent sees the reawakening of the whole Carnival with an accession of joyous life.

This is the day of the Great Festival, called the *Domingo de Pinatas*, the Sunday of the Kettles. The rabble has changed costumes and the streets swarm with red, blue, green, yellow or pink tatters, which were once mosquito nettings, curtains, or women's skirts, and which now serve as insecure daytime garments for the small brown bodies of yelling bands of urchins. They gather from all sections in noisy battalions, flourishing scraps of cloth at the end of a stick, and with lusty shrieks scamper about the streets under the protective anonymity of masks, their eager sparkling eyes peering through the two holes. "Anda! Hombre! Que no me conoce!" they cry, and the adult population is quick to step aside before this terrible masked invasion.

The windows are alive with innumerable dusky heads. All the young girls from the country have come to Seville for that day, and they carry fans that cast a pale bluish shade on their piquant powdered features. Confetti, like brightly coloured snow, flutters over everything. The narrow streets ring with cries, shouts, and merry laughter. Inhabitants and visitors, numbering only a few thousand in all, create more tumult on this day than could all Paris.

The carnival of Seville came to a close in 1896 on the 23rd of February, the Sunday of the Pinatas; and André Stévenol was conscious of a slight feeling of vexation, for the week of romantic license had not yielded, for him, a single new adventure.

His several visits to Spain had taught him

how casually and whole-heartedly the knots were formed and untied in this still primitive land, and he was depressed by the fact that chance and opportunity had not proved favourable. True, a young girl with whom he had engaged in a furious battle of serpentines from the window to the street, had descended running, after beckoning to him, to offer a small red bouquet, with a "*Muchisima' grasia', caballero*" in a strong Andalusian accent; but she had retreated with such precipitation, and she had seemed, moreover, so disillusioning at close range, that André was content to stick the bouquet in his lapel without fixing the woman in his memory. And, after this, his day appeared more empty than before.

Twenty different churches pealed forth the hour of four. He left Las Sierpes, walked past the Giralda and the ancient Alcazar, and along the Calle Rodrigo, a Champs-Elysees of shadowy trees beside the immense Guadalquivir which was crowded with vessels. There the more fashionable element of the city abandoned itself to the Carnival.

In Seville, the finer class is not always rich enough to afford three meals a day; but it would rather fast than dispense with that ostensible luxury which lies in the possession of a landau and two perfect horses. The small provincial city numbers fifteen hundred private carriages, often outmoded, but acquiring such glory from the beauty of the animals,

[165]

and distinction from the noble countenances
of their occupants, that none would dream of
ridiculing the frame.

André Stévenol made his way with the
greatest difficulty through the mob which
bordered both sides of the large dusty avenue.
The scene was dominated by the cry of the
youthful vendors, "Huevo'! Huevo'!" Here
the Battle of Eggs was in progress.

"Huevo'! Quiere quiere huevo'! A do'
perra' gorda' la docena!" Hundreds of egg-
shells which had been emptied, filled again with
confetti, and then stuck together with a tiny
band, were heaped in yellow wicker baskets.
They were thrown with full force, like play
balls, threatening the faces which passed in the
slow carriages. Standing on blue seats, the
caballeros and the *senoritas* replied to the dense
crowds, sheltering themselves behind small
plaited fans. André, who had provided himself with a quantity of these harmless pro-
jectiles, fought with renewed spirit.

It was a battle of some excitement and risk,
for while the eggs never wounded anyone,
they struck with real force before bursting
into coloured snow; and André became aware
that he was throwing them with more vigour
than was really necessary. Once he even
splintered a fan which had a brittle shell. But
how out of place a ball-room fan actually
was in such a scuffle! He continued with un-
hampered relish.

One after another the carriages rolled by, filled with women, lovers, families, children or friends. André regarded this happy company, parading amidst a riot of laughter and sunshine. Several times his eyes caught and held other admirable eyes; for the young girls of Seville did not lower their eyelids before such glances, but accepted the homage as their due.

The game had now lasted an hour, and André decided that it was time for him to retire. With a hesitating hand, he was rolling the last egg in his pocket when he suddenly caught another glimpse of the young woman whose fan he had broken.

She was indeed marvellous.

Deprived of the shelter which had for a time protected her laughing face, and now entirely exposed to attacks from the crowd and from those in the carriages, she had sprung up in her seat, and, standing erect, panting, with dishevelled hair, flushed with the heat and frank joy, she counter-attacked.

She looked about twenty-two years old, which means that she must have been perhaps eighteen. That she was an Andalusian there could be no doubt. She belonged to that race, unique among all, which derives from the mixture of Arabs with the Vandals, the Semites and the Germans, and which unites in an exceptional manner all the contrasting perfections of these dissimilar types.

Her tall and supple body was strangely expressive. Her thoughts, one felt, would burn through any veils with which she might mask her face; and she seemed to smile with her legs as she spoke with her torso. Only women who do not become immobilized near the fire in the long northern winters have that grace and that freedom. Her hair, a dark chestnut in colour, seemed at a distance to be nearly black, as it lay like a heavy shell over the nape of her neck. Her soft, rounded cheeks seemed powdered with that rare bloom which one observes on the skin of creoles. The thin border of her eyelids was naturally dark.

The pressure of the crowd had pushed André almost to the steps of her carriage, and he gazed at her for a long time. He smiled, became conscious of his agitation, while the rapid beating of his heart told him that this woman was one of those who would vitally affect his life.

He lost no time in acting on his impulse, realizing that at any moment the flow of carriages, which had momentarily stopped, might start again, and she would be lost to sight. Stepping back as far as possible, he took from his pocket the last egg, wrote rapidly in pencil on the white shell the six letters of the word *Quiero* and, choosing an instant when the eyes of the fair unknown were fixed on his, he gently threw the egg, in an upward sweep, as if it were a rose. Deftly the young woman caught it in her hand.

Quiero is an astonishing verb which can mean anything: such as *wanting, hoping, loving,* or, possibly, *inviting,* and also *cherishing.* It expresses the most compelling passion or the lightest caprice, according to the tone given it. It is a command or a prayer, a declaration or a condescension. Sometimes it conveys only irony. André's look, accompanying the throw, signified simply: "I would love to love you."

As though comprehending that the shell contained a message, the girl slipped it into a small leather bag which hung from the front of her carriage. No doubt she would have turned in acknowledgment had not the current of the procession taken her swiftly towards the right and, other vehicles intervening, André lost sight of her before he could follow her carriage through the crowd.

He broke through the throng as best he could, left the sidewalk, and ran towards a cross alley. But the multitude which crowded the avenue, did not allow him to act quickly enough, and when he succeeded in climbing on a bench where he could see over the battle, the young head he was looking for had disappeared. Discouraged, he returned through the streets. For him the light had gone out of the whole Carnival.

Bitterly he blamed himself for the awkward fatality which had cut his adventure short. Might he not have penetrated to the first ranks of the crowd, if he had been more prompt and resourceful? . . . . . Where now could he find the incomparable woman? He was not even certain that she lived in Seville. If unhappily, she did not, how could he search for her, in Cordova, in Jerez, in Malaga? Such an enterprise would be futility itself.

And slowly, by that poignant illusion that sways all human experience, the lost image became more than ever enchanting. Characteristics which might have received only passing attention, became, in his recollection, the principal motive for his thwarted adoration. He recalled that instead of allowing two curls to lie flat on her temples, she had coaxed them with the curling iron into twin rounded shells. Not a very original fashion, it is true, and one that many girls of Seville followed, but evidently *their* tresses did not lend themselves so charmingly to the cunning of those rounded curls, for André did not remember having seen any, even at a distance, that were in any way comparable to these. Moreover, an astonishing mobility could be discerned in the corners of her lips. Their form and expression changed each instant: sometimes almost invisible and sometimes almost curled up, round or thin, pale or dark, animated with a restless flame. The other features could be criticized certainly; the nose was not Greek nor was the chin Roman. But it was inconceivable that a man would not blush with pleasure when confronted with the two little capricious corners of this mouth.

He was preoccupied with these troubled musings, when a rough voice, shouting "*Cuidao!*" caused him to jump into an open doorway. A carriage was passing at a slow progress in the narrow street. And in this carriage was a wonderful girl, who, s e e i n g André, threw very gently, as if it were a rose, an egg which she had been holding in her hand.

It fell rolling, luckily, and did not break; for André, quite dazed at this unexpected re-meeting, had not been quick enough to catch it. The carriage had already turned the street corner when he stooped to pick up the envoy.

The word *Quiero*, nothing more, was still legible on the round, smooth shell; but a vigorous flourish, which might have been engraved by the point of a brooch, elongated the final letter as though converting it thereby into an answer.

II

*Wherein the reader becomes acquainted with
certain diminutives of the Spanish
given name "Concepcion"*

Only the remote clatter of the horses' hoofs
resounded on the cobblestones in the direction
of the Giralda, when André started in pursuit.
He was determined not to miss this second
opportunity which might be the last, and he
caught up with the carriage just as the horses
slowly entered the shadow of a pink house in
the Plaza del Triunfo.

The large black grating opened to admit a
quick feminine silhouette, and closed again,
definitely.

Undoubtedly it was the part of wisdom to
assure himself of his ground, to ascertain her
name, family, character, and position, before
rushing headlong into a chance intrigue, where,
as he knew nothing, he was master of nothing.
Nevertheless, André's eagerness would not permit him to leave the place without at least
having made a first effort. As soon as he had
adjusted the angle of his hat and the position
of his necktie, he boldly rang the bell.

A young steward appeared behind the
grating, but made no move to open it.

"What does your Excellency desire?"

"That you give my card to the senora."

"To what senora?" asked the servant, whose quiet voice maintained an admirable balance between suspicion and deference.

"To the one who lives in this house."

"But her name?"

André was too irritated to think of a ready reply. The servant continued:

"Will your Excellency do me the favour of informing me to which senora I shall present him?"

"Your mistress," said André, in a stern tone, "is waiting for me."

The steward, bowing slightly, lifted his hands, to show that it was not possible; and he retired without opening, or even taking André's card.

Goaded by anger into discourteous action, André rang a second and a third time, as one does at the door of a shopkeeper. He told himself that a woman who is so quick to answer a declaration from a stranger, should not be affronted at his insistence on entering her house; she was alone at the Delicias—she must live alone here and the noise he was making was heard, probably, only by her. He forgot that the Spanish Carnival sanctions passing indiscretions which could not be successfully pursued in normal life. The door remained non-committal, and the house as silent as though it were deserted.

What now remained for him to do? He

paced for a while on the spot before the windows, where he hoped to see the awaited face appear and give him, perhaps, a sign. . . But nothing happened; he resigned himself to going back. Nevertheless, before leaving a door which shut in so many mysteries, he noticed, not far away, a pedlar of wax matches sitting in a shady corner. He spoke to him:

"Who lives in that house?"

"I don't know," answered the man.

André put ten *reales* in his hand and added: "Nevertheless, tell me."

"I should not tell. The senora buys from me, and if she learned that I babbled about her, tomorrow her *mozos* would buy somewhere else; for instance, from Fulano, who sells half-empty boxes. At least I shall not speak evil of her, *caballero!* Only her name, as you wish to know it. She is the Senora Dona Concepcion Perez, wife of Don Manuel Garcia."

"Her husband, then, does not live in Seville?"

"He is in Bolivia."

"Where is that?"

"Bolivia is a country in America."

Without further questioning, André tossed another coin at the vendor, and rejoined the crowd to return to his hotel.

He was, on the whole, unsatisfied. Even in the absence of the husband, he did not believe that all the chances leaned in his favour. The caution of the pedlar, who probably knew

[174]

more than he cared to say, implied the existence of another lover already chosen; and the behaviour of the steward did not belie the suspicion of mental reservations. . . . Only fifteen days remained to André before he would be obliged to return to Paris. Could he, in this short time, insinuate himself into the good graces of a young person whose life was in all probability already occupied?

Torn by doubt and perplexity, he was about to enter the patio of his hotel, when he was stopped by the porter:

"A letter for your Excellency."

The envelope had no address.

"Are you sure this letter is intended for me?"

"It was handed to me this instant for Don André Stévenol."

André opened it without further pause.

On blue note-paper was inscribed this brief message:

"Don André Stévenol is kindly begged not to create a disturbance, not to give his name, and also not to ask for mine. If, tomorrow, towards three o'clock, he will walk along the road to Empalme, a carriage may pass that way, and perhaps may stop."

"How simple life is!" exulted André.

Climbing the staircase to the first floor he was already wrapped in visions of future intimacies, and in endearing variations on that most charming of given names: *Concepcion, Concha', Conchita, Chita.*"

III

*How and why André failed to go to the
Rendezvous of Concha Perez.*

It was a radiant awakening for André Stévenol the next morning. Light streamed prodigally through the four windows of the room; and all the city noises, the clamping of horses' hoofs, the pedlars' cries, the mule-bells and the chimes of the convents, mixed their lively uproar in the white square.

Not for a long time had he opened his eyes upon such a happy morning. He stretched his arms vigorously, then drew them in against his chest, as though to give himself the illusion of the anticipated embrace.

"How simple life is!" he repeated, smiling. "Yesterday at this hour I felt myself alone, without aim, without plan. A walk was enough—and this morning there are two of us. Why should we consider refusals, disdain, or even delays? We ask and women consent. Why should it be otherwise?"

He arose and put on a robe, then rang for his bath. While waiting, he leaned against the window pane and looked down into the brilliant square.

The houses that met his gaze were painted in those light colours, resembling women's

[176]

dresses, which Seville delights to spread over her walls. Some were of dazzling cream colour with white cornices; others pink, but of such delicate rose tints! Others were aquamarine or light orange and others pale violet. Nowhere were the eyes shocked by the horrible brown of the streets of Cadiz, or Madrid; nowhere were they blinded by the hard whites of Jerez.

On the square, the orange trees were loaded with fruit, fountains gurgled, young girls were laughing, holding their shawls by the edges as Arab women close their *haick*. On every hand, from the corners of the square, from the middle of the carriage-way and the depth of the narrow streets, sounded the tinkling mule bells. It did not seem possible, to the musing André, that a man could live elsewhere than in Seville. After dressing, he slowly drank a small cup of Spanish chocolate and then went out at random.

By some chance he followed the shortest way, from the steps of his hotel, to the Plaza del Triunfo; but once there, André, remembering the caution he had received, and not wishing to offend his fair unknown by passing too close to her door, or not caring to appear too eager with desire to see her sooner, followed the opposite sidewalk without even turning his head to the left. From there he walked over to *Las Delicias*.

The battle that had raged the day before

had strewn the ground with papers and egg-shells which gave to the splendid park the aspect of the back of a kitchen. In places, the earth had disappeared under crumbling, multicoloured dunes. Otherwise it was deserted, for Lent had begun. Then he espied a stroller who was e m e r g i n g from an alley leading to the country.

"Don Mateo, good day!" he said, offering his hand. "I had no hope of meeting you so soon."

"What is one to do when one is alone, useless and idle? I walk in the morning, I walk in the evening. D u r i n g the day I read or gamble. That is my life. It is a dreary one."

"But you have nights which make up for the days, if I am to believe the gossip of the city."

"If they still say that, then they speak falsely. From now until the day of his death, no woman will be seen again at the house of Don Mateo Diaz. But enough about myself. How long are you going to stay here?"

Don Mateo Diaz was a Spaniard, of some forty years, who had been recommended to André on his first visit to Spain. Like many of his countrymen, he was naturally declamatory in his gestures and his words, according an extreme importance to passing observations. But this characteristic carried with it no implication of vanity or stupidity. The Spanish emphasis, like the cape, is c a r r i e d in large, graceful folds. Don Mateo was a man of culture, whose excessive wealth had excused him from following any regular occupation and he was famed for nothing so much as the exploits of his bedroom, which was reputed hospitable. Andre was surprised, therefore, to learn that his friend had so soon renounced all the pomps of all the satans. But he refrained from further inquiries.

They walked for a while along the banks of the river which Don Mateo, as riparian proprietor and true patriot, never wearied of admiring.

"You recollect that joke," he began, "of the foreign ambassador who preferred the Mazanares to all the other rivers, because it was navigable by carriage and on horseback? Look at the Guadalquivir, the father of the plains and the cities! I have travelled a great deal in the last twenty years, I have seen the Ganges, the Nile and the Atrato, larger rivers under a more vivid light; it is only here that I have seen the majestic beauty of the current and the waters. Its colour is incomparable. Is it not gold which flows from the arches of that bridge? The stream swells like a woman with child. It is the wealth of Andalusia which the two quays of Seville lead to the plains."

Then they discussed politics. Don Mateo was a royalist and felt indignant at the persistent efforts of the opposition. He thought that all the forces of the country should have concentrated around the frail and courageous queen in her attempt to save the supreme inheritance of an imperishable history.

"What a fall!" he exclaimed. "What misfortune! To have possessed Europe, to have produced Charles V, to have enlarged the horizon of the world by discovering a new continent, to have ruled an empire over which the sun never set; and, even better, to have been the first to vanquish your Napoleon,—and then to fall under the blows of a handful of mulatto bandits! What a destiny for our Spain!"

It was vain to tell him that those bandits were the brothers of Washington and of Bolivar. To him they were low brigands who did not even deserve the garrote. He composed himself and continued:

"I love my country, its mountains and plains; its language, its costumes, and the sentiments of its people. Our race is essentially superior in quality. She herself is an aristocracy, apart from Europe, unaware of all that is not herself, and sheltered in her lands as within the walls of a park. That is without doubt the reason for her decline to the profit of the northern nations, according to contemporary law which everywhere impels the mediocre to assault the best... You know that in Spain they call the descendants of families who are free from any mixture of Moorish blood, *hidalgos*, refusing to admit that during seven centuries Islam took root on Spanish soil. It has always seemed to me ungracious to deny such ancestors. We owe entirely to the Arabs those exceptional qualities which have drawn in history the great design of our past. To us they bequeathed their scorn for material wealth, their disdain of lies, of death, their inexpressible pride. From them we inherit a rigid intolerance of everything that is low, and likewise an unaccountable laziness toward physical effort. In truth we are their sons, and it is not without reason that we continue to dance their Oriental dances to the tune of their 'ferocious songs'."

The sun was rising in a great expanse of blue sky. The brown masts of the old trees in the park revealed, at intervals, the green of laurels and of supple palms. Enchantment seemed to rise in the sudden puffs of heat that emanated from this winter morning in a land where no winter dwells.

"You will lunch with me, I hope?" suggested Don Mateo. "My *huerta* is near the road to Empalme. It is but half an hour's walk and, if you can spare the time, I shall detain you until evening to show you my breeding stud and some new animals."

"The luncheon I accept gladly," said André, "but I must be so rude as to leave shortly afterwards. This afternoon I have a *rendezvous* which is one that cannot be missed, I assure you."

"A woman? Don't fear, I shall ask no questions, but release you in plenty of time. I

[181]

am even grateful for your passing with me the time which must elapse before the appointed hour. At your age, I could not bear to see anyone during my mysterious days. I had my meals served in my room and spoke with no one from the time of my awakening until I greeted the expected woman."

After a short silence, he continued in an admonitory tone.

"My friend, beware of women! I shall never counsel you to avoid them, for after a life wasted in their company I can say that the only hours I should wish to live again are those gilded by love. But beware, beware of them!"

And, as though this thought were the key to a treasure-house of others, Don Mateo added more slowly:

"There are two kinds of women who should be avoided at all costs: the women who rule you, and the women who submit to you. Between these two extremes, there are thousands of charming creatures, but we do not know how to appreciate them."

Luncheon would have been a pretty dull affair, if Don Mateo had not filled in, by a long and animated monologue, the pauses which occurred in the conversation. André, preoccupied with his private speculations, gave only half his attention to what was said. As the anticipated moment drew near, the accelerated heart beats which he had felt the day before started again with a most painful insistence. It was an imperative call within himself, a driving impulse which cleared his mind of every thought except the intoxicating one that he was soon to see this peerless woman. He looked repeatedly at the large hand of the Empire clock as if he wished to push it forward fifty minutes. . . But the hour we await becomes fixed and time flows no more than an eternally stagnant pool.

At length, unable any longer to endure the tension of the crawling moments, he confessed his youthfulness by speaking thus to his host:

"Don Mateo, I have always found you an excellent adviser. Will you permit me to impart a confidence and ask your counsel?"

"I am at your disposal," said Mateo in the Spanish manner, rising from the table to go to the smoking room.

"Well . . . there . . . there is a question . ." said André in a hesitating voice. "Really, to anyone but you I would not mention it. . . Do you know a girl of Seville who is called Dona Concepcion Garcia?"

Mateo started.

"Concepcion Garcia! Concepcion Garcia! Which one? Explain yourself! There are twenty thousand Concepcion Garcias in Spain! Jeanne Duval or Marie Lambert are not more common in your country. Tell me her maiden name, for the love of God! Is it P . . . Perez, tell me? Is it Perez? Concha Perez? Why don't you speak?"

André, thoroughly startled by this sudden outburst, had a passing premonition that it would be better not to reveal the truth; but he spoke sooner than he had intended, exclaiming:

"Yes."

Mateo, accenting each syllable as one prods a wound, continued: "Concepcion Perez de Garcia, 22 Plaza del Triunfo, eighteen years, dark hair, and a mouth . . . a mouth. . ."

"Yes," . . . said André.

"It is well that you have asked me about her, senor; it is well. If I can stop you at her door, it will be a merciful deed on my part and a rare happiness for you."

"But who is she?"

"What? Is it possible you do not know?"

"I have not yet heard her voice; I met her yesterday for the first time."

"It is not too late, then."

"Is she a woman of the town?"

"No, no. She is even, in fact, an honest woman, and has not had more than four or five lovers. In our day that is chastity."

"But. . ."

"Beside that, she is extraordinarily intelligent, believe me. Remarkably. Her wit is of the subtlest, and in knowledge of life I do not know her equal. There is no praise that I can deny her. She dances with an eloquence which is irresistible. She speaks as she dances and she sings as she speaks. You have noted, no doubt, that she has a pretty face; and if you saw what she hides, you would admit that even her mouth... But enough of that. Have I covered everything?"

André, irritated, made no answer.

The other seized him by the two sleeves of his coat, and, emphasizing each word with a jerk, he added:

"And she is the *worst* of women, do you hear? She is the *worst* woman in the world. I have only one cherished hope, one consolation to my heart, that on the day of her death, God will not forgive her."

André arose.

"Nevertheless, Don Mateo, I, who am not authorized to speak of this woman as you do, cannot decently withdraw from the *rendez-vous* which she has granted. I know it is not necessary to repeat that I have placed a confidence in you and that I regret to cut short your explanations by a premature departure."

And he held out his hand.

Don Mateo, placing himself against the door, besought him as follows:

"Listen to me one moment, I beg of you. Hear me. A moment ago you addressed me as a man of excellent counsel. I do not accept that judgment. I do not need it in order to speak to you in this manner. I also forget the affection I bear towards you and which, nevertheless, would be sufficient to explain my insistence."

"But then? ..."

"It is as one man to another that I speak, as the first comer would stop a passer-by to warn him of a grave danger ahead, and shout, 'Go no further; return, forget whom you have seen, who has spoken to you, who has written to you!' If you now enjoy peace, calm nights, a carefree life, all that we know as happiness, do not go to Concha Perez! If you do not want this day to divide your past from your future as two halves of joy and suffering, do not go near Concha Perez! If you have not yet felt to the utmost the madness which she can inspire and hold in a human heart, do not go near that woman; flee from her as from death; let me save you from her. At least, have pity on yourself!"

"Don Mateo, do you love her?"

The Spaniard rubbed his hand over his creased brow and muttered:

"No, no, everything is over. I neither love nor hate her. The affair is past. Everything wears away. . ."

"You are sure that I would not be hurting you personally if I disregarded your advice? A sacrifice of that kind I would gladly offer you; but for myself I have none to offer. . . What is your answer?"

Mateo returned André's look. Then, with a sudden alteration of expression, he said in a whimsical tone:

"Anyway, one should never go to the first *rendezvous* a woman gives."

"Why?"

"Because she herself will not come."

André, remembering a particular incident, could not help smiling as he said:

"That is sometimes true."

"Often, very often. And if, perchance, she is waiting for you at this moment, be sure that your defection would only deepen her inclination for you."

André paused, reflected, and smiled again.

"What, precisely, do you mean?"

". . . I mean that without going into any personalities, and if your young woman's name were Lola Vasquez or Rosario Lucena, I would still recommend that you resume your seat and not leave it without a serious reason. We are going to smoke cigars while drinking iced syrups: a mixture that is not familiar to the restaurants of Paris, but which is known from one end of Spanish America to the other. Later you will tell me if you relish the fragrance of an Havana mingled with cool sugar."

A short silence fell. Soon they were sitting at a table which held *puros* and round ash trays.

"And now, what shall we talk about?" said Don Mateo.

André's answering gesture signified plainly: You know well.

"I will begin, then," said Mateo in a low voice; and his assumed gaiety of a moment before evaporated before the recurring gloom of his expression.

[187]

IV

In which a black imp dances across a polar landscape.

Three years ago, my friend, the white hairs which you see now had not yet appeared in my head. I was thirty-seven years old, and I still felt twenty-two; at no time of my life had I been conscious of my passing youth, and no one, as yet, had made me feel that it was gone.

You have been told, and falsely, that I was a libertine. On the contrary I respected love so much that I never frequented the back-shops, and I have s c a r c e l y ever possessed a woman whom I did not passionately love. If I were to name them, you would be astonished, perhaps, at their small number. Once I made a mental inventory, and discovered that I had never had a blonde sweetheart. I shall always regard indifferently those pale objects of desire.

The truth is that love has never been, for me, a dissipation, a game, or a pastime, as it is for some. It has been my whole life. To dismiss from my remembrance those thoughts and actions which concerned woman would be to leave nothing but a blank.

This being made clear to you, I pass on to tell you what I know of Concha Perez.

It all happened three years ago; three years

[188]

and a half, this winter. I was returning from France one 26th of December, during a terrible cold snap, in the express which, toward noon, passes over the bridge of La Bidassoa. The snow, already thick in Biarritz and Saint Sebastian, continually obstructed the passage of the Guipuzcoa. The train halted two hours at Zumarraga, while workmen hastily shoveled the drifts from the tracks. Then it started, only to stop again among the mountains, where it took three hours to repair the damages of an avalanche. This was repeated at intervals throughout the long night. The window panes were heavily lined with snow which smothered the noise of the t r a i n while we rode in the midst of a silence which gave a certain dignity to the danger.

The next morning there was a stop at Avila. We were eight hours late, and had not eaten for an entire day. I asked an e m p l o y e e if we could d e s c e n d ; he shouted: "Four days stoppage. The trains cannot pass."

Do you know Avila? People who believe that old Spain is dead should be sent there. My trunks were carried to a *fonda* where Don Quixote might have lodged; men in fringed trousers sat around f o u n t a i n s ; and, in the evening, when calls in the streets informed us that the train was about to start at once, the coach, drawn by black mules which carried us at a gallop through the snow and almost turned over a score of times, must assuredly have borne, in an earlier day, the subjects of King Philip V from Burgos to the Escorial.

What I take but a few minutes to relate lasted forty hours. When, towards eight o'clock in the evening, I sat down in my corner, still without my dinner, I felt myself overpowered by an immeasurable boredom. I could not endure the thought of passing a third night in the compartment with four sleeping Englishmen with whom I had travelled all the way from Paris. I left my grip in the upper section and, carrying my blanket with me, I sat down as best I could in an inferior compartment which was filled with Spanish women.

Rather I should have said four compartments, for all communicated at breast height. There were women of the lower class, some sailors, two nuns, three students, a gypsy and a civil guard. It was, as you see, a general mixture. They spoke all at once and in high shrill voices. Fifteen minutes of this had not passed before I knew something of the lives of all my neighbours. Some laugh at people who are so lacking in reticence. For my part I can never watch, without a sensation of pity, this need of simple souls to voice their pains in the desert.

The train came to a sudden stop, as we were passing through the Sierra de Guardarrama, at a height of fourteen hundred metres. Another avalanche barred our way. The train tried to back out; another slide blocked its return. And the snow continued slowly burying the cars.

This sounds like a story from Norway, does it not? If we had been in a Protestant country, the people would have knelt down to recommend their souls to God's keeping; but except during thunder-storms, our Spaniards do not fear the vengeance of h e a v e n. When they heard that the train was definitely blocked, they asked the gypsy to dance for them.

She danced. She was at least thirty years old, and, like most of the women of her race, very ugly, but seeming to have fire between her waist and her calves. She had barely started when we forgot the cold, the snow, and the darkness. Those of the other compartments were on their knees on the wooden benches, their chins on the barrier, looking at the gypsy. Those nearest to her, clapped their palms in cadence according to the ever varying rhythm of the *baile flamenco*.

It was then that I became aware of a little girl in the opposite corner who was singing. She wore a pink skirt, and this fact made me guess that she was Andalusian, for the Castilian women prefer strong colours, the French black, and the German brown. Her shoulders and her childish breasts were covered by a cream-coloured shawl, and, as a further protection against the cold, she had wound about her head a white foulard which ended behind in long horns. The whole waggon knew already that she was a pupil of the convent of

San José d'Avila, that she was going to Madrid to her mother, that she was innocent, and that her name was Concha Perez. She had a singularly clear voice. Her hands were under her shawl, and she sang without moving, almost prone, with closed eyes; but the songs which she sang she had not learned from the nuns, I thought. She chose well among the coplas of four verses wherein the people pour out their whole passion. I can still hear her voice, which had in it a thrilling note of caress:

> *"Your coverlets are jasmines,*
> *Your sheets are roses white,*
> *Your pillows lilies, and yourself*
> *A rose asleep at night."*

I give you only the less lively portions.

Then, suddenly, as though perceiving how absurd it was to address such hyperbolas to that wild woman, she suddenly struck a new vein, and began to accompany the dance with such ironic verses as this one:

> *"Little one with twenty lovers*
> *(And the twenty-first am I)*
> *If of my mind are the others,*
> *All alone I think you'll lie."*

At first the gypsy was undecided whether to laugh at these jibes, or r e s e n t them. The humour of the company was with the little one, and it was plain that this daughter of

Egypt did not possess that gift of repartee which, in our day, replaces livelier combats. She ground her teeth but did not retort.

The child grew bolder with these assurances of impunity, and the audacious gaiety of her attack redoubled. Then she was stopped by an outburst of wrath, and the sudden advance of the Egyptian with lifted, twitching hands:

"I will tear out your eyes, you. . .! I will tear out. . ."

"Ah! I must be very careful," remarked Concha, in the coolest manner imaginable, and without even lifting her eyelid. Then amidst an hurricane of abuse she called out in a calm, authoritative voice;

"Guards, bring me two *chulos*,"[1] as though she were confronted by a bull.

The whole compartment was ready to shout with joy. The men yelled *Ole* and the women looked at her with tender eyes. Only once did she falter; that was when the gypsy flung at her the biting taunt:

"Little bitch!"

"I am a woman!" cried the little one, beating her budding breasts.

And the hot-blooded pair threw themselves at each other with real tears of rage. I interfered; fist fights between women I have never been able to watch with the callous indifference of the mob. Women fight unfairly and

---

[1]Bullfighters' assistants.

dangerously. They do not know the clean knock-down blows, and they must needs assault each other with their murderous nails and teeth, dealing scars and deformities. They frighten me.

Separating them was a difficult task, and I realized the foolhardiness of interfering between two violent enemies. But I did my best, and had the satisfaction of seeing them finally throw themselves into opposite corners, fuming with impotent anger.

When all was quiet, a lanky lout dressed in the uniform of the civil guards emerged from a nearby compartment, climbing over the wooden barriers with his tall boots. He looked around the peaceful battle-field in a protective manner and, with that unfailing instinct of the police which causes them to victimize the weakest, he struck poor little Conchita's cheek a senseless and brutal blow.

Not condescending to explain the summary sentence, he banished the girl to another section, returned to his own, climbing back in his absurd boots, and then crossed his hands over his sword, with the air of an efficient guardian of the public peace.

The train was once more under way. We passed Santa Maria de las Nieves in an enchanting landscape. The fairy radiance of the frozen moon ravished the snowy Sierras, more divine on that winter night than I have ever seen them. Snow and moon gleamed back at each

other, rivals in dazzling whiteness. It was easy
to fancy oneself riding in a silent and fantastic caravan towards the discovery of a new
world.

I was the sole witness of this stupendous
spectacle. My neighbours were already asleep.
Have you ever, dear friend, marked the fact
that people never look at anything beautiful?
Last year on the bridge of Triana, I had stopped
to watch at leisure the most magnificent sunset I had seen that year. Nothing can really
convey an idea of the splendour of Seville
at such a moment. Yet the passers-by were
hastening along in a bored, uneasy fashion; not
one turned his head, not a single person shared
with me that glorious drama. . . As I drew in
the beauty of the night and the snow, the
image of the little singer crossed my mood,
and I smiled at the incongruity. That little
black-headed imp in this stark landscape was
like a mandarin on an iceberg, a banana at the
feet of a white bear, a droll anomaly.

Where was she now? I peered over the
barrier and saw her close to me, so close that
I could have touched her. She slept soundly,
her mouth open, her hands crossed under her
shawl; her head had slipped down on the arm
of the nun. She might indeed be a woman, I
told myself, but she slept like a six-months-old
child. Most of her face was wrapped in her
foulard which clung about her cheeks. I could
see nothing more than a round and dark wisp

[195]

of hair, an eyelid closed on very long lashes, a small nose in the light and two lips marked by s h a d o w s. Nevertheless, I gazed at this singular mouth until dawn, wondering at its childish and sensual curves, and whether, in her dreams, the movements of her lips sought a nurse's breasts or the mouth of a lover.

Daylight appeared as we passed the Escorial. The dry and dull winter of the *alrededores* had succeeded, in the frame of the windows, the wonders of the Sierras. Soon we entered the station, and, as I carried my bag on the platform, I heard a young voice shouting:

"Mira! Mira!"

She was p o i n t i n g with her finger to the masses of snow which covered the roofs of the train, from one end to the other, stuck to the windows, the buffers, the springs, the ironwork; and, compared to the clean trains which were leaving the city, the mournful appearance of ours made her burst out laughing. I helped her with her many parcels, and wanted to find someone to carry them for her, but she refused. She had six of them, and these she quickly distributed, one to her s h o u l d e r s, another to the crook of her elbow, and the other four in her two hands. Then she darted off, at a run, and I lost sight of her.

You see, senor, what a vague and insignificant meeting ours was. Unlike the orthodox opening of a novel, the setting took more space than the heroine, whom I might have overlooked entirely. But that is the way it really b e g a n, oddly, inconsequentially, like most adventures in real life.

I could swear to you now, that if anyone had asked me, on that morning, to name the principal event of the night, the memory that would r e m a i n with me out of those forty hours, my answer would have been, not Concha Perez, but the landscape.

Her antics had a m u s e d me for twenty minutes; and the tiny image reappeared once or twice in my m i n d, then the current of events carried me elsewhere, and I did not think about her any more.

v

Wherein the same person re-appears in another setting.

I met her again the following summer in a very unexpected manner. I had returned to Seville some time before, had resumed an old *liaison*, and had already broken it. Of this I shall not tell you; it is not a series of memoirs that I am giving you, and, beside, intimate confessions are distasteful to me. But for the strange coincidence which unites us around a woman, I would not have shown you this fragment of my remembrances. This confidence should at least remain the only one between us.

In the month of August, I found myself alone in my house which for years had been graced by a feminine presence. The second place was no longer laid at the table, the wardrobes were empty of gowns, the beds lonely, and the silence depressing. If you have been a lover, you will understand me: it was horrible. To escape from this mourning, the worst of mournings, I stayed away from dawn to dark, not caring where, or how I went, on horseback or on foot, carrying a gun, a stick or a book. I even slept at an inn sometimes, to avoid the empty horror of my house. One afternoon, my aimless wanderings led me to

the Fabrica,[1] which, for lack of something
better to do, I decided to explore.

It was one of those overpowering summer
days. I had lunched at the Hotel de Paris and,
going from Las Sierpes to the street of San
Fernando, "at the hour when only dogs and
Frenchmen are found in the streets", I thought
I would perish from the relentless heat.

By special favour, I entered alone. As you
know, visitors are usually guided by a female
superintendent through that immense harem
of four thousand eight hundred women, who
are so free in their dress, behaviour, and speech.
On this day, which was torrid, as I have said,
these women availed themselves fully of that
privilege which allows them to leave off as
much clothing as they please in the intolerable
atmosphere in which they must live from June
to September. This rule is dictated by simple
humanity, for the temperature in these long
close rooms is like that of the desert, and it is
only charitable to permit those poor girls the
same liberty given to firemen on steamships.
The result, as you can imagine, is not less interesting.

The most prudish among them had only a
chemise draped around their bodies. Most of
them worked with the torso nude, and a simple
cotton skirt hanging loose around the waist,
sometimes allowed to drop half-way down the

---

[1]Tobacco factory in Seville.

thighs. It was a diverting scene. Women of all ages met the gaze, childish and old, young or less young, obese, sturdy, slim or emaciated. Some were pregnant. Others nursed their babies. Some were not even nubile. One could see every type in that frankly exposed crowd, except, probably, virgins. There were even pretty girls.

Between these serried ranks I passed, looking from right to left, sometimes solicited for alms, sometimes affronted with the most cynical jests. For the appearance of a man, walking alone in this prodigious army of women, excites many emotions. They do not spare their words when they have dropped their garments, and to their provocative speech they add gestures of a shamelessness, or rather of a simplicity, which is somewhat disconcerting, even to a man of my age. They are fully as immodest, I assure you, as respectable women. I did not wait to answer all of them; for who can flatter himself that he has had the last word with a *cigarrera*? But I looked at them attentively and found that their nakedness did not agree with the idea of painful work. I fancied that I saw all those active hands devotedly manufacturing innumerable little lovers out of tobacco leaves. Their appearance and manner suggested as much.

It was indeed a strange contrast between the poverty of their clothing and the fastidious care they had bestowed on the heavy hair

which weighted their heads. They had dressed
it with curling irons as though in anticipation
of a ball, and had powdered themselves to the
tips of their b r e a s t s, even over their holy
medals. There was not one that I could see
without forty pins and a scarlet flower in her
coiled tresses. Not one who did not carry,
folded in her handkerchief, a small mirror and
a white powder puff. They could have passed
for actresses in the disguise of beggars.

I considered them singly, and saw that
even the shyest among them betrayed some
consciousness at being examined. There were
young girls, children almost, who placed themselves at ease, as if by chance, as I approached.
I gave some *perras* to those who had babies; to
others bouquets of pinks with which I had
filled my pockets, and which they immediately suspended by the little chain attached to
their crosses. There were, to be sure, some very
poor anatomies in that anomalous herd, but
all were interesting; and more than once I
s t o p p e d in front of an admirable feminine
body. Truly, it is only in Spain that one can
find that warm torso, full of flesh, velvety as
a fruit and quite sufficiently covered by sparkling skin uniformly dark, from which springs
vigorously the curly astrakan of the armpits
and the dark c o r o n e t of the breast. I saw
fifteen who were really beautiful. Among five
thousand women that is a great many.

By this time I was almost deafened, and not

a little tired. I was about to leave the third room, when I heard, near me, among the shouts and uproar of many tongues, a high pitched voice calling to me:

"Caballero, if you will give me a *perra Chica*[1] I will sing for you a little song."

I recognized, in utmost amazement, the voice and figure of Concha. I can see her now. She wore a long chemise, rather shabby, which hung from her shoulders and covered her scantily. She stood regarding me, with her hand moving among a sprig of pomegranate flowers in the first roll of her black hair.

"How," I asked her, "did you get here?"

"God knows, I don't remember."

"But your convent in Avila?"

"When girls return there by the door, they go out by the window."

"And is that the way you came out?"

"Caballero, I am honest. I did not go back at all for fear of committing a sin. Give me a *real*[2] and I will sing you a *soledad* while the superintendent is at the other end of the room."

You can probably picture the blaze of eyes that were focussed upon us during this short dialogue. I felt somewhat ill at ease, but Conchita was undismayed. I continued:

"With whom are you staying in Seville?"

"With Mama."

This made me shudder. For a young girl, a

---

[1] One cent.
[2] Two cents.

lover is still a guarantee, but a mother—what perdition!

"We keep busy, Mama and I. She goes to church and I come here. That is the difference of age."

"Do you come here every day?"

"Almost."

"Only. . .?"

"Yes, when it does not rain, when I am not sleepy, when it does not tire me to walk. One comes here as one wishes—ask my neighbours —but one must be here by noon, otherwise one cannot enter."

"Not later?"

"Do not laugh. Noon! *Dios mio!* How early that is! I know some who, two days out of four, cannot get up early enough to reach the place while the grating is open. And, for that matter, for all that one earns here, one might as well remain at home."

"How much do you earn?"

"Seventy-five *centimes* for a thousand cigars and a thousand packages of cigarettes. As for me, as I work fast, I can earn a little piece, but that is not the wealth of Peru. . . . Give me a little piece, caballero, and I shall sing for you a *seguedilla* that you do not know."

I threw a napoleon in her box and, after pulling her ear, left her.

There is in the youth of happy people, senor, a certain moment when chance reverses itself, the ascent becomes a descent, and the season of misfortune is at hand. That was my critical moment. The golden coin thrown to that child was the fatal play of my life. From then I date my present life, my moral ruin, my degradation, and all the changes that you see marked on my brow. You shall hear it all, a very simple story, really almost banal, except in one point; but that one killed me.

I had left the factory and was walking slowly down the glaring street, when I heard little running steps behind me. I turned; she had joined me.

"Thank you, caballero," she said.

I noticed that her voice had changed. The effect of my little gift on her, which I had not foreseen, was profound. A napoleon is equal to twenty-four *pesetas*, the price of a bouquet; for a *cigarrera* it represents a month's work. Beside, it was a gold coin, and gold in Spain is only seen in the front windows of money changers. . . .

By my careless act, I had evoked all the emotion of wealth. She had, of course, quickly left the packages of cigarettes which she had been filling since morning; had resumed her skirt, her stockings, her yellow shawl, her fan; and, after hastily powdering her cheeks, she had pursued me.

"Come," she continued, "you are my friend. Take me back to my mother, as I am free now, thanks to you."

"Where does your mother live?"

"Calle Monteros, quite near. You have been nice to me, but you did not stay to hear my song. That is bad. To punish you, you shall tell me one."

"No, no, anything but that."

"Yes, I will prompt you."

She essayed to reach my ear, and "prompted" me as follows:

> *Do any others hear us?—No.*
> *Then shall I tell you?—Tell.*
> *You have another lover?—No.*
> *You wish to have me?—Yes.*

"But, you understand", she c o n c l u d e d, "that it is a song, and the answers are not mine."

"Is that the truth?"

"Entirely."

"But why?"

"Guess."

"Because you do not love me."

"But I find you very charming."

"Because you have a lover?"

"No, I have none."

"Because of piety?"

"I am very pious, but I have made no vows, caballero—"

"Then it is because of coldness, no doubt?"

"No, sir."

"There are many questions which I may not ask, my dear little girl. If you have a reason, pray tell me."

[205]

"I knew that you would not be able to guess.
It would be impossible to guess."

"But what is it, after all?"

"I am *mozita*."[1]

---

[1]Virgin.

VI

*Wherein Conchita makes a confession, a
stipulation, and a disappearance.*

Her tone was one of such simplicity and
assurance that I paused, in some perplexity.
What was the mental life of the mutinous and
provocative imp? What did this determined
attitude, this frank and perhaps open glance,
this sensual mouth, tempting in its very un-
approachableness, all portend? My thoughts
were confused, but I understood perfectly that
she pleased me very much, that I was delighted
to have f o u n d her again, and that I would
probably seize every pretext to observe her life.

We had now arrived at the threshold, where
a vendor of fruit was unloading her baskets.

"You will purchase some mandarins for
me?" she suggested. "We shall eat them upstairs."

I followed her up the stairs of a puzzling
house. The card of a w o m a n without profession was nailed at the first door. Above, a
flower-maker plied her trade. On the side was
a barred apartment from which issued happy
laughter. The question whether this girl was
not leading me merely to a most commonplace
adventure struck me for the first time. But
the surroundings contributed nothing to my

enlightenment. The poor *cigarreras* did not choose their dwelling-places, and it is not well to judge others by the name of their street.

When we had reached the top floor, she stopped on a landing bordered by a wooden balustrade, and k n o c k e d three times on a brown door which opened readily.

"Mother, here is a friend," said the girl. "Let him enter."

The mother was a faded dark woman who still retained some claims to beauty. She regarded me attentively, but without great confidence. I could not help feeling that the little daughter, who pushed the door so assuredly and invited me to follow her, was actually the mistress of that hovel, and that the queen-mother had abdicated her regency.

"See, mother, twelve mandarins! No, look again; a napoleon."

"Jesus!" ejaculated the elder, crossing herself. "And how did you earn that amount?"

Quickly I sketched for her our two meetings, once in the train and once at the Fabrica, and drew the conversation into the realm of intimate confidences. These threatened to become endless. The woman was, (or so she said), the widow of an engineer who had died in Huelva. She had come back to Spain without a pension, and without means of support other than the savings of her husband, which dwindled in four years of careful living. Whether the story was true or invented I could not tell; certainly

I had heard the same thing twenty times, and always terminated, as now, with a cry of misery.

"What could I do? I had no profession, I could only keep our little home and pray to the Holy Mother of God. I had been offered the place of a door-keeper, but my blood would not permit me to sink so low. All my days are passed in church. I have chosen the better part: to kiss the stones of the choir rather than sweep those of the door; and I wait for the Lord to reward me at the last moment. Ah, caballero, two lonely women are so unprotected! Temptations never shun those who are needy. We could live in luxury, my daughter and I, if we had listened to evil words. But sin has never found a shelter here. Our souls are straighter than the finger of Saint John and we put our trust in God, who knows His own among all the multitude."

Conchita, meanwhile, in front of a mirror nailed to the wall, had accomplished with two fingers and some powder, a work in pastels over all her little, too-brown face. She turned now, smiling brightly at what she had done, and it seemed to me that her mouth had blossomed into new life.

"What anxiety for a mother," resumed the woman, "to see her leave in the morning to go to the Fabrica! What bad examples they set her! What evil words they teach her! Those girls have no carmine on their cheeks, caballero.

One never knows where they come from when they enter in the morning; and if my daughter had listened to them, she would have left me long ago."

"Then why do you send her there?"

"Elsewhere it is the same. You know how it is, caballero; when two working women are twelve hours together, they speak of things that should not be mentioned, for eleven hours and three-quarters, and the rest of the time they are quiet."

"If it is only talk that passes between them, there is not much harm done."

"Who gives the bill-of-fare incites the appetite. Believe me, it is the whisperings of women more than the eyes of men that lead these girls from paths of virtue. I do not trust the best of them. Many a girl with her rosary in her hand has the devil in her bodice. I would wish, for my daughter, no woman friend either young or old. And there she has the pick of five thousand."

"Well, then," I interrupted, "don't let her go back any more."

And I took two bank notes from my pocket and placed them on a table; followed exclamations, clasped hands, and tears. That I pass over. But, when the outcries had ceased, the mother deplored, with a shake of the head, that the girl would nevertheless have to return to her work, as that sum and more was owing to the landlord, the grocer, the druggist, and

the clothier. In the end, I doubled my do-
nation and left at once, forbearing, both from
modesty and calculation, to express my sentiments at that time.

. . . . . .

But I cannot deny that it was before ten
o'clock when I knocked at their door on the
following day.

"Mother is away," explained Concha. "She
is at market. But come in, my friend!" Then
she resumed, with a little laugh. "Ah, well!
I am discreet before my mama. What would
you say?"

"That you are indeed."

"It is not the result of rearing, believe me.
I have brought myself up; which is well, as
my mother was quite incapable of the task.
I am good and she brags about it; but should
I stretch myself over the window-sill and hail
the passer-by, she would also admire me, saying
"Que gracia!" So I please myself the whole
day long. The credit is mine, then, that I do
not do everything that passes through my head,
for she is not the one who would restrain me,
in spite of what she says."

"Then, my little girl, when a *novio* shall
present himself for approval, it is to you he
must come?"

"Quite so. Do you know one?"

"Oh, no."

I sat facing her, in a wooden arm-chair of which the left arm was broken. I see myself still, my back to the window, near a ray of the sun which striped the floor. . . ."

Suddenly she sprang upon my knees, grasped my shoulders with her two hands, and said:

"Is that true?"

My arms had instinctively tightened about her, and my hand pulled toward me her dear face, which had grown so serious; but she anticipated my desire, and impulsively placed her burning mouth on mine, with a long deep look. Strange and unpredictable! Thus she has always been. The unexpectedness of her yielding intoxicated me like strong drink. I drew her closer. Her body molded itself to mine; I felt the softness and warmth of her legs beneath the thin stuff of her skirt. Then she got up.

"No," she said. "No. No. Go away."

"Yes, but with you. Come."

"Follow you? And where, pray? To your house, perhaps? My friend, you do not expect that."

I sought to embrace her again, but she shook herself free.

"Do not touch me, or I shall call out, and then we won't see each other any more."

"Concha, Conchita, my little one, are you mad? What do you mean? I came here as a friend, I spoke to you as a stranger. Then, without warning, you throw yourself into my arms, and now you cry out against me?"

"I kissed you because I love you well; but you may not possess me without loving me."

"And do you think, child, that I do not love you?"

"Yes, caballero; I please you, I amuse you. But am I the only one? Many girls have black hair, many pass in the street with eyes like mine. There are, at the Fabrica, many girls as pretty as I am, who would listen to you. Do what you will with them, I shall, if you wish, give you their names; but as for me, I am myself and there is no other like me from San-Roque to Triana. And I cannot be bought like a doll at the bazaar; for, once carried away, no one will find me again."

Footsteps ascended the stairs. Concha went to the door and opened it for her mother.

"Senor has come to inquire about you," said the girl. "He thought you did not look well."

An hour later, I left them, feeling unstrung and irritated, and in some doubt whether I should ever return. To my lasting sorrow, I did return, not once but thirty times. I was as fatuous as a young man. You know those follies well. You feel them now, as I am speaking to you, and you understand my emotions. Each time that I left her room I repeated in secret: "Twenty-two hours, or twenty hours, until tomorrow." And those twelve hundred minutes were always laggards.

Very soon, I began to remain all day long with them. I paid all their expenses and even their old debts, which must have been considerable, if I judge by what they cost me. That, however, was a recommendation in her favour and, beside, there was no gossip in the district. I was easily convinced that I was the first friend of these poor unprotected women. It did not take long to become intimate with them, but is a man ever astonished at the quick favours he obtains? A suspicion would have put me on my guard, but I did not stop to think about it; that is to say, about the lack of mystery and constraint towards me. There was never a moment that I might not enter their rooms. Concha was always affectionate but always reserved, and made no difficulties about allowing me to witness her dressing.

Sometimes she was still in bed when I came, as she got up later since leaving her work. Her mother would go out and she, moving her legs over in the bed, would invite me to sit beside her joined knees. Then we would talk. She was unfathomable. I have seen, in Tangiers, Moorish women in costume, who, between their two veils bared only their eyes, but through those I saw deep into their souls. This one concealed nothing, neither her life nor her form, yet I always felt a wall between us.

She appeared to love me. Perhaps she did love me. Even today I am not sure. To all my pleadings she responded with a "later" which I could not break. If I pretended to leave her, she answered, "Go away." If I threatened her with violence, she said simply: "You could not." I loaded her with presents; she accepted them, but with a gratitude always conscious of its limits. Yet in spite of all, when I entered her rooms, there was a light, not entirely artificial, that leaped to her eyes.

She slept nine hours each night and three hours in the middle of the day. Otherwise, she did nothing. She arose in the morning, only to stretch out in her wrapper on a clean mat, with two pillows for her head and a third one under her loins. She could never be tempted to any sort of occupation. Neither needle work, nor a game, nor a book had passed through her hands since the day when, through my own intervention, she had left the Fabrica. Even the household work did not arouse her. Her mother attended to the rooms, the beds and the meals, and every morning passed half an hour arranging the heavy hair of my little friend, still half asleep.

One whole week she refused to leave her bed. Not that she feigned illness, but she had decided that it was useless to walk in the streets without any destination, and even more absurd to take three steps in her room or to leave the sheets for the matting, where stiff clothes interfered with her repose. All our Spanish women are like that. To those who see them in public, the fire in their eyes, the vibrance in their voices, the quickness of their movements, seem to issue from a source in perpetual eruption; and yet, when they are alone, their lives flow with that smoothness which is their great sensuality. They stretch out in an easy chair in a room with lowered s h a d e s; they dream of the jewelry they could own, of the palaces they could inhabit, of the unknown lovers whose dear weight they might feel on their breasts. And thus their lives pass dreamily on.

In her conception of daily life Concha was truly Spanish. But from what country she had drawn her idea of love, I cannot say. After twelve weeks of assiduous care, I found in her smile the same promises and the same resistance.

Finally, one day, unable to endure any longer this perpetual waiting and this ceaseless preoccupation which troubled my life to the extent of making it empty and futile during the three months that it had lasted, I approached the old lady, while her daughter was absent, and opened my heart to her in the most urgent manner.

I confessed that I loved her daughter and had resolved to unite my life to hers; that for reasons easy to understand, an open *liaison* was out of the question but that I could and did offer her an exclusive and deep love which would repay the gift of her heart and confidence.

"I sincerely believe," I submitted in conclusion," that Concepcion would love me, but that her distrust will not permit it. If she does not love me, I have no intention of forcing her; but if my only misfortune is to have left her in doubt, then reassure her." I added that, in return, I would assure not only her present life, but her personal fortune for the future. And, to leave no doubts as to the sincerity of my promises, I gave the woman a thick roll of bank notes, as I implored her to use her maternal wisdom to persuade the girl that she would not be deceived.

I returned to my house, wildly excited. All that night I did not sleep. For hours I walked through the patio of my house; the air was cool and refreshing but not sufficiently so to calm me. I had high hopes for the success of a solution that had seemed sound to me, and I formed endless plans. At sunrise, I ordered all the flowers of three bushes to be clipped and these I scattered on the walks, on the stairs, on the *perron*, to make a path of purple and saffron for her dear feet. I saw her everywhere: against a tree, sitting on a bench, lying on the lawn, leaning behind the balustrades, or raising her arms in the sun towards a fruit-laden branch. The soul of the garden and the house had become incarnate in her body. After a whole night of intolerable suspense and a morning which s e e m e d eternal, I received through the mail, towards eleven o'clock, a letter of a few lines. Believe me that I know it from memory. She had written me this:

"If you had loved me you would have waited

for me. I wished to give myself to you, but you have asked that I be sold. We shall never meet again."

Ten minutes later, I was on horse-back, and midday had not struck when I a r r i v e d at Seville, almost o v e r c o m e by the heat and anguish. I bounded up the stairs and knocked twenty times. Silence. Finally a door opened behind me on the same landing, and a neighbour explained, in answer to my questions, that the two women had left that morning in the direction of the station, with their parcels, and that no one knew even what train they had taken.

"Were they alone?" I was barely able to ask.

"Quite alone."

"No man with them? You are sure?"

"Jesus! I have never seen any man but you in their company."

"Did they leave anything for me?"

"Nothing; if I am not mistaken they were angry with you."

"But will they come back?"

"God knows. They did not say."

"Surely they will return to get their furniture."

"No, the house was furnished. They have taken all that they owned. And by now, senor, they are far away."

VII

*Wherein a promise and an ornamental
tail-piece are drawn with black hair.*

The autumn and the winter wore drearily
away, but my painful remembrances remained
undimmed. I can recall no period of my life
so arid as that one. I had thought I could enjoy a loving intimacy with Concha for a long
time, perhaps for life, but my fragrant hopes
had withered prematurely, and every day the
ruin confronted and tortured me. I had not
even one hour of real union with her; not one
bond, not one accomplished act, nothing which
could comfort me, even by the vain thought
that, if she was lost to me forever, at least I
had possessed her, and this could not be taken
away from me. . . .

My God, how I loved her! How I loved
her passes all belief. It was such a love as soon
began to taunt me with the thought that her
treatment of me was not without reason and
that I had behaved like a boor with this legendary virgin. "If I ever see her again," I would
swear to myself. "if Heaven favours me in this
one thing, I shall crouch at her feet until she
makes a sign, even if years pass over my head.
I shall precipitate nothing. How could I have
been insensible of her feeling? She knows her-

self to be in a condition which exposes her to the subtle arts of the seducer, and she does not wish to incur a treatment unworthy of her real value. She wants to test me, to be sure of me and, if she gives herself, it will not be as a loan. So be it; I shall be all that she desires. But," and here my anguish overwhelmed me once more, "shall I see her again?"

I saw her again. It was in spring, in the evening. I had whiled away a few hours at the Theatre del Duque, where the perfect Orejon played several rôles, and, emerging in the cool stillness of the night, I walked for a long time in the spacious and deserted Alameda. I was returning alone, smoking a cigar, when I heard my name called in a soft voice. I trembled suddenly as I recognized its unforgotten tones.

"Don Mateo!"

I turned, but saw no one. I could not feel that I had imagined those tender accents.

"Concha!" I cried, "Where are you, Concha!"

"*Chito!* Speak quietly, or you will wake mama."

I saw her now through a grilled window, the stone of which was at the height of my shoulders. She was in her night-dress, her arms covered with a gray shawl, and she leaned against the marble, behind the iron bars.

"Well, my friend! Is that the way you regarded me?" she resumed in a low voice.

I had no spirit for defending myself. . .

"Lean over," I said to her. "A little lower, dear love. I cannot see you in that shadow. A little more to the left, in the moonlight."

She complied silently and I looked at her in absolute intoxication for an immeasurable length of time. At last I said:

"Give me your hand."

She gave it to me through the bars and I trailed my lips over the fingers, in the palm, along the naked, warm arm, in a kind of frenzy. I could scarcely believe it was her skin, her flesh, her fragrance; all of her which I held there under my kiss, after so many sleepless nights! Then I begged her:

"Give me your mouth."

But she shook her head and withdrew her hand.

"Later."

Ah, that word! How many times had I already heard it from her lips, and now it cast a chill over this long hoped-for reunion that reached my very soul.

I plied her with questions now. What had she been doing? Why that hurried departure? If she had spoken to me I would have obeyed. But to run away in that cruel fashion after a simple letter!

"It was your fault," she answered.

I admitted it, as, indeed, I would have admitted anything. And I kept silent. Then I broke out afresh. What had she been doing during those long months? Where did she come from? How long had she lived in that grilled house?

"We travelled first to Madrid, then to Carabancel to visit relatives. From there we came here."

"Do you occupy the whole house?"

"Yes, it is not large, but it is still too much for us."

"And how were you able to rent it?"

"Thanks to you. Mother economized on everything that you gave her."

"That will not last long. . ."

"We still have enough to live here comfortably for another month."

"And then?"

"Then? Do you seriously believe, my friend, that I shall be embarrassed?"

I was silent; inwardly, with all my heart, desiring to kill her. She went on:

"You misunderstand me. If I wish to remain here I shall know what to do, but who tells you that I am so eager about it? Last year I slept for three weeks under the walls of La Macarena. I lived there, on the ground, near the corner of the street of San Luz, you know, where the *sereno* keeps himself; he is a good man, he would not have permitted anyone to approach me during my sleep, and nothing ever happened to me, except adventures in words. I could return tomorrow. I know my clump of grass; it is not uncomfortable there, I assure you. During the day I could work in the Fabrica or somewhere else. I could sell bananas, no doubt! I can knit a shawl, weave ornaments for skirts, make up a bouquet, dance the *flamenco* and the *sevillana*. Don't worry, Don Mateo, I shall be all right."

Her voice was subdued, yet I heard each of her words ring like the words of an oracle in the empty, moonlit street. I listened to her less than I watched the moving double line of her lips. Her voice tinkled like the clear music of convent chimes. Still leaning on her elbows, her right hand lost in her heavy hair, and her head resting on her fingers, she began again with a sigh:

"Mateo, I shall b e l o n g to you after to-morrow."

I started trembling again.

"You are playing with me."

"I am telling you the truth."

"Then why not long ago, dear heart? If you had loved me. . ."

"I have always loved you."

"Then why not at this very hour? See how the bars have been bent from the wall. I could pass between them and the window."

"Sunday night you will pass. Tonight I am blacker with sin than a gypsy. I do not want to become a woman in this perditious state; my child would be cursed if I conceived by you. Tomorrow I shall confess all that I have done in the last eight days and even what I

shall do in your arms, so that he may give me
the absolution in advance; it is more certain.
On Sunday morning I shall communicate at
high mass and when I shall have in my breast
the body of Our Lord, I shall ask him to make
me happy in the evening and loved for the rest
of my life. Amen!"

Yes, I know quite well that it is a peculiar
religion, but our S p a n i s h women know no
other. They firmly believe that Heaven has
inexhaustible indulgences for all lovers who
go to mass and, when necessary, favours them,
watches over their beds, glorifies their flanks,
so long as they do not forget to relate their
cherished secrets. If, after all, they are right,
how many chastities will weep, during a life
eternal, over an insignificant earthly pilgrimage?

"And now, leave me, Mateo," said Concha.
"You can see that my room is empty. Do not
be impatient or jealous on my account. You
will find me here, my lover, Sunday, late at
night, but you must promise beforehand, that
you will never tell my m o t h e r and t h a t
you will leave me in the morning before she
awakens. I am not afraid to be seen: I am
my own mistress, you know. Beside, I have
no need of her counsel, either for you or against
you. Do you swear it?"

"As it pleases you," I answered.

"Very well, be bound by this."

And drooping her head, she let her hair

[224]

stream like a fountain of perfumes through the bars. I took it in my hands, I pressed it to my lips, I bathed my face in its warm, dark waves. . . Then it withdrew from my ardent caresses as Concha closed the heavy window.

VIII

*Wherein it becomes gradually clear who
is the puppet of this story.*

Two successive mornings I awoke with her
promise pulsing in my blood, two days I whiled
restlessly away, two nights I courted sleep, in
the interval that seemed endless. In this happy,
uneasy time, among the contradictory emotions
which possessed me, I was dominated by a sharp
apprehensive joy that revealed, like fitful
lightning, the anticipated aspects of "what
was going to happen."

An hundred times, during those forty-eight
hours, my mind projected the impending
wonder: the setting, the words, and even the
silences. I could not refrain from mentally
enacting the imminent rôle which awaited me.
I saw myself, I felt her in my arms. Over and
over again, the same scene, with inevitable
slight variations of incident, reproduced itself
in my exhausted imagination.

The hour arrived. I passed up and down the
street, not daring to stop under her window,
for fear of compromising her, and yet tor-
mented by the suspicion that she was watching
me from behind the panes, and deliberately de-
laying the moment for which I waited in a
smothering agitation.

She called me, at last.

"Mateo!"

Senor, at that instant I became as young as she. Behind me, twenty years of love resolved into a dimly remembered dream. I achieved the absolute illusion that for the first time I was going to press my lips to the lips of a woman and feel her young, warm body bend and lie heavy upon my arm. Like a stage lover, I lifted myself with one foot on a stone and the other upon the bent bars, and entered her room. I embraced her.

She stood with her body pressed against mine, abandoning herself and, at the same time, stiffening. Our heads, joined at the mouth, merged in the shadow, our nostrils panting, our eyes closed. Never did I understand so clearly as in the vertigo, the frenzy, the half-unconscious state in which I found myself, all that is really meant by the "intoxication of the kiss." I no longer knew who we were, nor how we had come there, nor what would befall us. The present was of such fiery intensity that in it were melted the past and the future. Her lips moved under mine, she burned in my arms, and her small stomach, through her skirt, pressed me in a shameless and fervent caress.

"I don't feel well," she murmured. "Wait, I beg of you. . . I think I am going to fall. . . . Come into the patio with me, I will lie on a fresh mat. . . I love you, but wait. . . I am near fainting."

I went towards a door, but she checked me. "Not that one. It is mother's room. Come this way. I will lead you."

A black square of starry sky with fleecy bluish clouds dominated the patio. The floor gleamed under the moon's rays, and the rest of the court lay in a confidential shadow.

Concha stretched herself, in her Oriental manner, on the matting. I sat near her and she took my hand.

"My friend," she said, "will you love me?"

"How can you ask that?" I demanded, fretfully.

"How long will you love me?"

I dread these questions which all women ask, and which can never be answered except with the sorriest banalities.

"Will you love me still when I shall be less beautiful?. . . When I am old, quite old, will you still love me? Tell me, my dear, even if you do not speak the truth. For I have need to hear you, to give me strength. I promised you for tonight, I know, but I am not certain that I shall have the courage. . . Nor do I know yet if you deserve it. O, Holy Mother of God! If I should be deceived in you, I think all my life would be lost. I am not one of those girls who go to Juan and Miguel and from them to A n t o n i o. After you, I shall never love another; and, if you leave me, I shall be as one dead."

She compressed her lips as if in pain, her eyes fixed on space; but gradually her lips relaxed in a smile.

"I have grown in the last six months. Already I cannot tighten my last year's corset. Open this one; you shall see how beautiful I am."

If I had begged her for this privilege, I should probably have been refused; I had begun to doubt whether this tender conversation would develop into a night of love; but when I did not touch her any more, she drew nearer. Alas! The breasts which rose to my view when I uncovered the swollen corset were fruits from a fabled land of delight. If there were any others as beautiful, I knew it not. Even these never again rivalled their own beauty on that night. Breasts have their youth, their flowering, and their decline. I believe even now that I saw Concha's during their flash of perfection.

During my mesmerized contemplation, she had taken from between these snowy peaks of beauty a scapulary in black cloth. She kissed it piously, watching my emotion from the corner of her half-closed eye.

"I please you, then?" she asked.

I folded her again in my arms, against her resisting motion.

"No, later."

"What is it now?" I asked, in despair.

"I feel disinclined, that is all."

And she closed her corsage.

I suffered atrociously. I supplicated her almost rudely, struggling with her hands which became defensive. I could have cherished her and maltreated her at the same moment. Her cruelty in luring me and then repulsing me, a repetition of those maneuvers which I had endured for a year and which redoubled at the supreme moment when I expected the accomplishment, wore out even my tenderest patience.

"My little one," I reasoned, "you are playing with me, but take care that I do not become tired."

"Indeed? Well, I shall not love you this evening, Don Mateo. Tomorrow."

"I shall not return."

"You will return tomorrow."

Furious, I put on my hat and went out, determined never to see her again. I kept my resolution firm up to the time of my sleep, but what a grey and heavy awakening mine was! I feel its weight upon me now, as I remember.

In spite of myself I took the road for Seville. I was drawn toward her by an invincible power, for my will had ceased to exist; I could no longer govern the direction of my steps.

Followed three hours of fever and inward struggling, as I wandered in the Calle Amor de Dios, behind the street where she lived, ever wavering on the point of encompassing the twenty steps that divided us. . . Finally I mastered myself and went away, almost at a run, without knocking at the window that sheltered her. But what a wretched victory! It was dry as dust in my mouth.

The next day she appeared at my door.

"You would not come to me," she said, "so I have come to you. Will you believe now that I love you?"

I longed to throw myself at her feet.

"Quickly, show me your room," she added. "Today you will not accuse me of reluctance. Would you believe that I am impatient, I also? You would be very surprised if you knew what I thought."

But, when she had entered, she recovered herself.

"No, really, not that one. There have been too many women in that wicked bed. This is not the r o o m for a *mozita*. Let us take another one, a guest room which belongs to no one. Will you?"

This delayed matters an hour. The windows had to be opened, the sheets changed, the floor swept. . .

At last everything was ready and we went upstairs. It would be over-emphatic to say that I was now certain of success; but at least my hopes were high. Knowing my feelings, it appeared unlikely that she would have risked herself in my house, alone, without protection, unless she had already arrived in her mind at the surrender she now offered me.

When we were alone, she loosened her man-
tilla, which was attached by fourteen pins to
her hair and to her corset; then, very simply,
she began to disrobe. I admit that, instead of
hastening the lengthy process, I rather held it
back, by interrupting her innumerable times
to touch with my lips her bare arms, her
rounded shoulders, her firm breasts, her tawny
neck. I watched her body appear, little by
little, to the edges of the underclothing, and I
was at last persuaded that this young rebel
flesh was to be mine in very fact.

"See, have I not kept my word?" she asked,
drawing her chemise tight to mould her supple
body. "Close the blinds; the light is unpleasant
here."

She sank silently in the deep bed, while I
obeyed her command. I saw her through the
mosquito netting, white as a stage apparition
behind a curtain of gauze. . .

And now, how shall I say it, senor? You
have guessed that this time also I was played
with and put to shame. I told you that this
girl was the most terrible of women and that
her cruel subterfuges passed all bounds; but
up to this point, perhaps, you have not fully
realized it. From now on, if you follow my
recital, scene by scene, you will begin to know
Concha Perez for what she really is.

She had come to me, she said, to offer herself. I have given you her loving words, her

promises. Up to the critical moment, she acted like an amorous virgin, who wished to know pleasure, almost like a young bride giving herself to her husband, a young married woman, not without knowledge, I must admit, but nevertheless serious and moved.

Well, while dressing herself at home, this remorseless wanton had put on drawers, made of a kind of canvas, so stiff and so strong that a bull's horn would not have penetrated it, and which she tightened about her waist and between her thighs by laces of an unassailable resistance and intricacy. And that is what I discovered in the midst of my most passionate fire, while the obscene wretch explained to me calmly:

"I shall be as foolish as God permits, but not as far as men desire."

For an instant, I thought I would strangle her. Then—really, I confess it, and am not ashamed —I buried my weeping face in my hands.

What I wept for was my lost youth which this girl proved to me, for the first time, was gone forever. Between twenty-two and thirty-five years there are o u t r a g e s which all men avoid. I cannot believe that Concha would have used me so had I been ten years younger. It seemed to me that, from then on, I would see those drawers, that barrier between myself and love, on all women; or that, at least, they would wish for them before approaching my embrace.

"Go away," I muttered. "I understand."

But at once she became alarmed, and, embracing me in her turn, with her two small but vigorous arms which I could hardly push aside, she said, while trying to reach my mouth:

"Dear heart, will you, then, never be able to love all that I give you of myself? You have my breasts, my lips, my warm legs, my scented hair, all my body in your embraces and my tongue in my kiss. Is it not enough, all this? Then it is not I you love, but only that which I refuse you! All women could give you that; why do you ask it of me, who resist? Is it because you know I am a virgin? There are others, even in Seville. I swear to you, Mateo, I know of them. Love me as I wish to be loved, a little at a time, and be patient. You know that I am yours, and that I keep myself for you alone. What more would you have, dear heart?"

It was arranged that I would see her at her house or at mine, and that all would be as she desired. In exchange for a promise on my part, she agreed never to wear that horrible canvas armour, but more than that I could not obtain from her; and truly on the first night when she did not wear it, my torture seemed to me even greater.

To this degrading slavery did that child reduce me. (I pass over the continual demands for money which interrupted her conversation and which I always granted; but even apart from that, the nature of our relations is of a particular interest.) Thus, each night I held in my arms the naked body of a girl of fifteen, without doubt brought up by the nuns, but of a condition and quality of soul which excluded any idea of bodily virtue—and this girl, otherwise as passionate and fiery as one could wish, behaved toward me as though nature herself prevented her from ever gratifying her lusts.

No excuses could be offered for such a comedy; none existed. You yourself will guess the reason later, and as for me, I permitted her to ridicule me so.

Do not deceive yourself, young Frenchman, reader of novels and perhaps an actor in particular intrigues with the demi-virginities of the watering places; our Andalusian women have neither the taste nor capacity for artificial love. They are admirable lovers but their senses are too keen to bear, without frenzy, the quivers of a false treble string. Between Concha and myself nothing happened, absolutely nothing. Understand what I mean by nothing. And this lasted two whole weeks.

The fifteenth day, after she had received from me the sum of a thousand duros to pay her mother's debts, I found her house deserted.

IX

*Wherein Concha Perez reappears for the fourth
time on the stage of these adventures.*

That second outrage gave me the shock I
needed. I now saw with appalling clearness
into that crafty little soul. I had been tricked
like a collegian, and there was more shame than
grief in the thought.

The humiliating episode was one that should
be dismissed as speedily as possible from my
mind; thus I recommenced the weary task of
endeavouring to forget her from one day to the
next, by a violent effort of will, one of those
paradoxical resolutions of which women always discount the inevitable miscarriage.

I experimented with the classic stratagem
which the whole world trumps up and which
always fails. I departed from Madrid with
the determination to take, by chance, for a
mistress, the first young woman who attracted
my eyes.

From drawing-room to drawing-room, from
theatre to theatre, I wandered with an eager
eye, and finally fixed upon an Italian dancer,
a large girl with muscular legs, who would
have been an ideal candidate for the seclusion
of a harem, but who lacked most of the qualities one requires in a particular and intimate

[236]

friend. She exerted all her pretty arts for me, was affectionate and compliant. She taught me the vices of Naples which were strange to me and which pleased her more than they did her pupil. I saw that she tried hard to keep me near her, and that anxiety for her material welfare was not the only motive that animated her.

Why could I not love her? Alas! There was no serious fault or flaw in her. She was neither faithless nor importunate. She did not seem to be aware of my defects. She did not make me quarrel with my friends. Furthermore, her fits of jealousy, as frequently as they occurred, merely suggested rather than expressed themselves. She was a priceless woman.

But I had no feeling for her.

For two months I f o r c e d myself to live under the same roof with Giulia, enduring her atmosphere, passing hours in her room in the house I had rented for us at the end of the Street Lope de Vega. She came in and went out, and I followed neither movement with my eyes, nor did I feel more than abstractedly conscious of her presence. Her skirts, her dancing tights, her drawers, and her chemises trailed their silken length over the divans; but their influence never reached me. For sixty nights, I saw her brown body stretched near mine in a bed too hot, where I imagined another presence as soon as the room was dark. . . Then I ran away, more wretched than ever for the remedy that had failed.

I came again to Seville. My house chilled me like a mortuary. I left for Granada, where I was bored; then Cordova, parched and deserted; then dazzling Jerez filled with the odour of wine cellars; then Cadiz, an oasis of houses in the sea.

In all this wandering I was guided from city to city, not by my will or fancy but an irresistible and distant fascination which I doubt no more than the existence of God. Four times in vast Spain I met Concha Perez. This could not have been the result of a series of accidents; I do not believe in those dice-throws which are believed to rule destinies. It was inevitable that that woman should seize my life again, and that I should see and feel all that I shall now tell you. And, in fact, everything was accomplished.

. . . . . .

It was at Cadiz.

One evening I entered the *Baile* of that place. I saw her there. She danced, senor, before thirty fishermen, as many sailors, and some stupid foreigners. As soon as my eyes fell on her I began to tremble. I must have been as pallid as earth; I was breathless and without strength. I sat down on the bench nearest the door, and, elbows on the table, I regarded her from a distance, like a dead man brought back to life.

[238]

She was still dancing, panting, heated, her face red, her breasts shaking, and rattling deafening castanets in each hand. I was certain that she saw me, but she gave no sign. Her *balero* ended in a gesture of furious passion, the challenge of her leg and her torso aimed by chance at anyone among the crowd of spectators. Suddenly she stopped in the midst of great clamour.

"*Que guapa!*" yelled the men. "Ole! Chiquilla! Ole! Ole! Otra vez!"

Their hats were tossed madly upon the stage; the whole crowd sprang to its feet, while Concha saluted, still breathless, with a little smile of triumph and of disdain.

As the custom was, she descended among the guests to sit at a table, while another dancer succeeded her behind the footlights. And knowing that there was, in a corner of that hall, a being who worshipped her, who would grovel at her feet before the whole world, and who suffered at this moment to the point of hysterics, she strolled from table to table, from arm to arm, unconcerned beneath the heat of his gaze.

They all knew her by name. The countless greetings of "Conchita!" made me shiver from head to heels. They offered her drinks, someone touched her naked arms, one, a German sailor, gave her a red flower which she stuck in her hair; she pulled the hair braid of a *banderillero* who acted like an ass; she feigned amorous interest in a young fop sitting with some women, and caressingly touched the cheek of a man whom I could have killed.

There was not a move or a gesture of hers during this interlude, which lasted fifty minutes, that has since left my memory. It is of such stuff that one's past is woven.

My table was at the end of the room, and she visited it last, as though in a natural order; but she came to it. Confused? In theatrical surprise? Not at all! You do not know her, senor. She sat down facing me, clapped her hands to attract the waiter, and cried:

"Tonio! A cup of coffee!"

Then, with an exquisite composure, she met and sustained my look.

I said to her in a very low voice:

"Are you afraid of nothing, Concha? Are you not afraid to die?"

"No! Anyway, it is not you who will kill me."

"Then you defy me?"

"Right here and where you wish. I know you, Don Mateo, as though I had carried you for nine months; better. You will never touch a hair of my head, and why should you? For I no longer love you."

"You dare to say, after all, that you ever loved me?"

"You may think what you please. You alone are to blame."

She reproached me! I might have expected

such posturing.

"Twice," I resumed, "Twice, you have deceived me! What I gave you from the bottom of my heart, you took like a thief and used as a means of leaving me without so much as a word, a message, w i t h o u t even directing someone to bring me your farewell. What have I done that you should treat me so?"

And I flung at her between my teeth:

"Wretch! Miserable wretch!"

She was as ready as ever with her justification:

"And you—what have you done? You deceived me, Mateo. Did you not swear that I was safe in your arms and that you would let me choose the night and the hour of my sin? Have you already forgotten the last time, when you thought that I was asleep, and could feel nothing? I was awake, Mateo, and the realization penetrated me that if I passed another night at your side, I would not escape without being delivered to you by surprise. And I was compelled to run away."

It was all too preposterous for rebuttal. I shrugged my shoulders, and said:

"So that is the basis of your c o m p l a i n t against me? In the face of what I see here: the kind of life you lead and the men who pass over your bed?"

In a flash she stood before me, outraged.

'That is not true! I forbid you to address me thus, Don Mateo! I swear on the grave of

[241]

my father that I am as virgin as a child. I swear, also, that I despise you because you have doubted me."

And I found myself alone. In a few minutes, I also left the place.

X

Wherein Mateo is taken behind the scenes.

I paced about the ramparts all that night. The eternal winds blowing in from the sea quieted my fever and my cowardice. Yes, I felt like a coward before that woman. The thought of my relations with her brought a burning blush to my cheeks. I heaped upon myself the worst insults one could address to a man. And all the time I foresaw that in the morning I would still deserve them.

A calm consideration of the whole matter suggested only three possible things to do: leave her, conquer her, or kill her.

I decided on the fourth one, the impossible thing, which was to endure her.

Every evening I took my place among the crowd, like a docile child, to watch her and to wait.

As time passed she softened towards me, little by little. That is to say, she forgave me for all the wrong she had done me. Behind the scenes there opened a large white hall where the mothers and sisters of the dancers waited and drowsed. Concha suffered me to stay there, which was the particular favour each of the young girls accorded her lover. A pretty gathering, you may be sure. The most distressing of my hours were passed there. You understand me, perhaps. I have never led that life of elbows on the table of low cabarets. I was horrified at my debasement.

Among the others, there was Senora Perez. She seemed ignorant of the occurrences in Calle Trajano. I did not know whether or not she was lying, nor did I worry about it. Instead, I listened to her confidences and paid for her alcohol. . . Of this I shall say no more.

The only joy I knew was during Concha's four dances, when I stood at the open door through which she emerged upon the scene; and, during the rare movements when she turned her back to the people, I experienced the fleeting illusion that it was for me alone she danced.

In the *flamenco* she achieved her greatest triumph. What a dance, senor! It is a very tragedy in inarticulate movement. It combines all the passions in three stages: desire, seduction, and enjoyment. No dramatic creation expresses female love with the intensity, the grace, and the fury of the three successive scenes. Concha was supreme in her interpretation. Do you really grasp its tremendous significance? To one who has not seen it I would have to explain in a thousand words. It is said that eight years are needed to make a *flamenca*, which means that, with the precocious maturity of our women, they have lost their beauty by the time they have perfected the dance. But not so with Concha. She was born a *flamenca;* more priceless even than experience, she had intuition. You know, of course, how it is danced in Seville. You have seen our best ballerinas, of which not one is perfect; for this exhausting d a n c e (twelve minutes! Can you find an Opera dancer who can go through a variation of twelve minutes!) has in it three unrelated rôles: the lover, the *ingenue* and the tragedian. One must be sixteen years old to act the second part wherein Lola Sanchez now realizes marvels of sinuous gestures and l i g h t attitudes. One must be thirty years old to play the end of the drama, wherein the Rubia, in spite of her wrinkles, is still excellent every night.

Concha is the only woman I have seen who is equal to the whole of the terrible performance.

I can always see her, advancing and retreating in a short balanced step, looking sideways under her lifted sleeve, slowly, with a movement of hips and torso, lowering her arm over which emerged her two black eyes. I see her, delicate or ardent, her eyes lively or bathed in languor, striking with her heel the boards of the floor or snapping her fingers at the end of her movement, as though to give the cry of life to each of her undulating arms.

As she stepped from the stage in a state of excitement and lassitude which made her even more beautiful, I see her now. Her flushed face was beaded with perspiration, and her sparkling eyes, her mobile lips, her young throbbing breasts, all transfigured her head and shoulders with a very halo of exuberance and undying youth. She was resplendent.

. . . . .

Matters continued in that way for a month. I was tolerated in the back shop of her theatrical platform, but was not allowed to escort her to her door. I kept my place near her only on condition that I never reproached her for the past nor worried her about the present. As to the future, I did not know what she thought about it; for myself, I had no idea of any solution to the pitiful adventure.

I understood that she lived with her mother in the only suburb of the city, near the Plaza de Toros, in a great white and green house which harboured also the families of six other ballerinas. I dared not imagine what happened in such a city of women. . . However, our dancers lead a very regular life; from eight o'clock in the evening until five in the morning they are on the stage; they go home, worn out, at dawn; they sleep, often alone, until the middle of the afternoon. They have only the end of the day which they might abuse; but the fear of a ruinous pregnancy restrains these poor girls who, moreover, could not be persuaded to add other fatigues to their laborious nights.

Nevertheless, it gave me some uneasiness to think about it. Two sisters, friends of Concha, had a younger brother who lived in their room or in that of neighbours and created gusts of jealous wrath which I perceived on a number of occasions.

I never learned the real name of this youth, but he was nicknamed *The Morenito*. Concha would call him to our table, feed him at my expense, and ask me for cigarettes which she stuck between his lips. To all my protesting words, she responded with a shrug or she spoke in a glacial manner which hurt me even more.

"*The Morenito* belongs to everybody," she said. "If I were to take a lover he would be mine like my ring; you know that, Mateo."

I was silenced. Rumours about Concha's private life represented her as impregnable; and my desire to believe this made me accept, even with confidence, rumours without foundation. I saw no man approach her with that peculiar look of the lover who meets again, in public, his companion of the previous night. I had quarrels on this subject, with pretenders whom I hindered, no doubt; but never with anyone who bragged of having known her. Often I tried to make her friends talk. The answer was invariably: "She is *mozita*. She is quite right."

Concha and I went through no form of reconciliation. On the contrary, she asked nothing, and granted me nothing. So joyous before, she became grave and silent. Of what was she thinking? What did she expect from me? It was futile to try to fathom her expression. I might as easily read the impenetrable eyes of a cat as see into the depths of her little soul.

One night, at a sign from the director, she left the stage with three other dancers and climbed up to the first floor; for a siesta, she told me. She often left like that for an hour without arousing my suspicions; for, no matter how false and lying she was, I believed her least word.

"When we have danced well," she explained, "they permit us to sleep a little. Otherwise we would be dreaming upon the stage."

This time, also, she had gone upstairs and, in order to get a breath of pure air, I had left the hall for half an hour. Returning, I met in the lobby a simple-minded dancer, nicknamed *The Gallega* who, on this night, was a little intoxicated.

"You are returning too soon," she said to me.

"Why so?"

"Conchita is still upstairs."

"I shall wait until she wakes up. Let me pass."

"Until she wakes up?" she echoed, without seeming to grasp my meaning.

"Well, yes; what about it?"

"But she does not sleep."

"She told me. . ."

"She told you that she went to sleep? Oh, well!"

I could see her efforts to restrain herself. But, in spite of her tightly pinched lips, she burst out laughing.

I felt suddenly sick.

"Where is she? Tell me at once!" I demanded, seizing her arm.

"Don't hurt me, caballero. She is showing her navel to the *Ingles!*[1] God knows I cannot help it. If I had thought, I would not have told you anything. I do not want to have any trouble, caballero; I am a good girl."

Can you believe me? I remained impassive. But a great cold penetrated me, as though a breath from a cave had glided between my clothes and myself. My voice did not tremble as I commanded her:

"Gallega, take me upstairs."

She shook her head obstinately.

I resumed:

"No one will know that you have told me. Hurry. . . She is my *novia*, you understand. . . I have a right to go to her. . . Lead the way." And I placed a napoleon in her hesitating hand.

A moment later, I was alone on the balcony of an interior court and, through the French window, I saw, senor, a scene from hell.

I was looking into a second dancing hall,

---

[1] The name Ingles (English) is used to designate all foreigners in Spain.

smaller, well lighted, which contained a platform and two guitar players. In the centre,
in plain view, was Concha, naked, attended
by three other nude women, dancing a mad
jota before two Englishmen sitting in the back.
. . I said naked; she was worse than naked.
Black stockings, as long as dancers' tights, were
drawn up to her thighs, and she wore noisy
little shoes which stamped smartly on the floor.
I dared not enter. I was afraid I would kill her.

Senor, as God hears me, I had never seen her
so beautiful. Beauty that no longer confined
itself to her eyes or her hands, darted like a
flame from her whole body, which was itself
as expressive as a face, and more so. Her head,
swarming with her loose black hair, rested on
her shoulders like a superfluous provocation.
Smiles glanced from the folds of her hips,
there were blushing cheeks when she turned
her flanks; her breasts seemed to look forward
through two great eyes, fixed and dark. I
repeat it: never have I seen her so beautiful.
The false folds of a dress change the whole
expression of the dancer, deviate absurdly the
exterior line of her grace; but there, by a revelation, I saw the gestures, the shivers, the
movements of the arms, the legs, of the supple
body and the muscular loins, born indefinitely
from a visible source, the very centre of her
dance, the little brown belly.

I forced in the door.

To look at her for ten seconds and swear

to myself that I would not kill her, was the limit of my endurance. And now nothing could restrain me.

Piercing cries announced my invasion. I walked straight to Concha and said briefly:

"Follow me. Fear nothing. I shall not hurt you. But delay at your peril!"

Did she obey me? Ah, no! she f e a r e d nothing. She leaned against the wall and there extended her arms on both sides.

"I shall no more leave this place than Christ left the cross," she cried, "and you are not going to touch me, for I defy you to advance farther than that chair. Leave me, madame. You others, go downstairs. I have no need of you; I will attend to him."

XI

How Concha undergoes a metamorphosis

We were left alone. The Englishmen had been the first to disappear. Senor, until that hour I would have denounced a man as a cowardly beast, if I had been told that he had beaten a woman. And still I wonder by what power I was able to control my rage in front of her. My fingers opened and closed as if to strangle a neck. I was torn by the struggle between my anger and my will.

Ah! It is in such moments that one recognizes that woman's power is rendered supreme by the immunity with which we armour her. She insults you brazenly, she outrages you, and you bow to her. She strikes you; protect your skin, but take care she does not wound herself. She ruins you; let it be. She deceives you; say nothing about it, for fear of compromising her. She wrecks your life; kill yourself if you wish! But never, by any conscious act, let the slightest injury maim the flesh of those exquisite and ferocious beings in whom the pleasure of inflicting pain almost surpasses the capacity of receiving happiness.

The Orientals do not pamper them as we do, they who are the great voluptuaries. They cut their claws so that their eyes may be all

[252]

the sweeter. They master their malevolence the better to release their sensuality. I honour them.

But, in my power, Concha remained invulnerable.

I did not draw near to her. I spoke from the distance of three paces. She still stood against the wall, her hands crossed behind her back, her chest jutting out and her legs close together, straight in their long black stockings, like a flower in an ebony vase.

I began impatiently.

"Well, what have you to say to me? Come, invent! Defend yourself! Lie again; you can lie so admirably!"

"Ah, that is superb!" she retorted. "He accuses me. He enters here like a marauder through the window, smashing everything; he threatens me, he stops my dance, he evicts my friends. . ."

"Stop!"

". . . He may succeed in having me driven away from here; and it is my duty, then, to answer! It is I who have done wrong, is it not? I am the one who invited this ridiculous scene! Come, leave me; you are too stupid!"

And she took a towel from a drawer, with which she proceeded to rub herself from her navel to her head, absorbing a thousand pearls of perspiration which had gathered on her brilliant skin. I began again:

"Then this is what you are doing in this

[253]

very house where I see you! This is your life.
This is the woman I love!"

"Do you pretend, innocent, that you knew
nothing?"

"And how should I know?"

"How? That is good. Though all Spain
knows it; and all Paris and all Buenos Ayres;
though twelve-year-old children in Madrid tell
you that women dance naked in the first ball
at Cadiz, you, you would have me think that
no one had told you anything, you who are
a bachelor, you who are forty years old?"

"I had forgotten."

"He had forgotten! He has been coming
here for two months, he has watched me go
up to the small hall four times a week. . ."

"Be quiet, Concha, you make me suffer
horribly."

"But it is your turn now! I shall revenge
myself, Mateo, for what I have endured at your
hands tonight, for you have acted wickedly,
through an inconsiderate jealousy; and, I ask
myself, by what right? Who are you, anyhow,
to treat me so? Are you my father? No!
Are you my husband? No! My lover?. . ."

"Yes, I am your lover! I am that!"

She burst out laughing.

"Truly! You are satisfied with little."

I felt weak and sick again.

"Concha, my child, tell me, have you someone else? If you belong to someone, I swear
to you that I will leave you. You have only

to tell me that."

"I belong to myself and to myself alone. There is nothing more precious to me than my own self, Mateo. No one is rich enough to buy me from myself."

"But t h e s e m e n who were here a while ago. . ."

"Well, what of them? Do I know them?"

"Is that really true? You don't know them?"

"But no, I do not know them. Where do you think I would have met them? They are *Ingles* who have come with an hotel guide. To-morrow they leave for Tangiers. I am not at all compromised, my friend."

"But here? Not even here?"

"Look you, is this a bedroom? Look all over the house, is there a bed here? And you saw them, Mateo. They were d r e s s e d like mannikins, the hat on the head and the chin on the cane. You are crazy, I tell you; crazy to create such a scandal when I deserve no reproach from you."

Even had her defence been more childish, I think it would have persuaded me. I had such need of forgiving her! I feared only to learn the truth about her.

A last question still trembled on my lips; a last answer I must have to relieve me of torment.

"And *The Morenito?* . . . Tell me the truth, Concha. This time, I must know. Swear to me that you hide nothing from me, that you

[255]

will tell me all, if there is aught to tell. I
beseech you, my little girl!"

"*The Morenito?* . . . He was in my bed this
morning."

For a moment I was senseless, then my arms
closed on her, and I embraced her, not knowing, myself, whether I intended to smother her
or snatch her away from some i m a g i n a r y
person.

She understood and, laughing, exclaimed:

"Let me go, Mateo! You are dangerous just
now. You will take me by force in a fit of
jealousy. Good, now stay where you are; I
shall explain. . . My poor friend, there is no
reason for trembling as you do, I assure you."

"Are you sure?"

"*The Morenito* lives with his two sisters,
Mercedes and Le Pipa. They are poor. For
them and their brother, there is only one bed
which is not a large one. When it begins to
get hot, they prefer to sleep less crowded after
their dancing, and they send the boy to their
neighbours. This week mother is making the
Perpetual Adoration at the church; she is not
there when I am in bed; then Mercedes asked
me if I had room for her little brother and I
said yes. I do not see why this should disturb
you."

I looked at her without speaking.

"Yes" she resumed, "if that is all, you should
be c o n t e n t. I give him no more than his
sisters, you know. You can trust my word.

At the most, he kisses me a few times before going to sleep, and then I turn my back on him as though we were married."

She pulled the stocking on her right thigh and added slowly:

"As though I were with you."

The callousness, the audacity, or the rakishness of this woman, whatever one might call it, blunted all my feelings e x c e p t those of moral suffering. I was more u n h a p p y than irresolute; but unhappy to the point of tears. I took her very gently on my knees. She did not resist.

"Listen to me, Concha. . ." I began. "I can live no longer at your caprice, as I have been doing for a year. You must speak to me in all frankness and perhaps for the last time. I am horribly unhappy. If you remain another day in this dance hall and in this city you will never see me again. Is that your wish, little one?"

She answered, and in so new a tone that I thought I heard another woman speak.

"Don Mateo, you have never understood me. You believed that you pursued me and that I refused myself to you, when, on the contrary, it is I who love you and who want you for all my life. Remember the Fabrica. Were you the one who spoke first? Was it you who took me away from there? No. It was I who ran after you in the street, who dragged you to my mother's house and almost kept you by force, so afraid was I of losing you. And the next day. . . You recall that also? You came in. I was alone. You did not offer to kiss me. I can still see you, in the easy chair, your back toward the window. . . I threw myself on you, I took your head with my hands, your mouth with my mouth and—I have never told you —but I was quite y o u n g then, and it was during that kiss, Mateo, that I felt pleasure melting in me for the first time in my life. . . I was on your knees, as I am now."

I held her close, overwhelmed with emotion. She had reconquered me with a single pretty speech. She could always play with me as she liked.

"I have never loved any one but you," she continued, "since that night in D e c e m b e r when I saw you in the train, when I was leaving the convent of Avila. I loved you because you are handsome. You have such sparkling and tender eyes that it seems to me all women must love them. If you only knew how many nights I thought about those eyes. Later I loved you because you were kind. I would never have tied my life to that of an egotistical, handsome man, for you know that I love myself too well to accept being only half happy. I wished all happiness and I saw quickly that if I asked you for it, you would give it to me."

"But then, dear heart, why were you so long silent?"

"Because I am not satisfied with the things

that satisfy other women. Not only do I wish supreme happiness, but I want it for all my life. I want to marry you, Mateo, to keep on loving you when you shall love me no more. Oh, fear nothing; we will not go to the church, nor before the *alcalde*. I am a good Christian, but God protects sincere love, and I shall enter Paradise before many married women. I will not ask you to marry me in public for I know that cannot be done. . . You could never acknowledge Dona Concepcion Perez de Diaz, the woman who danced naked in this horrible den where we are, before all the *Ingles* who passed this way. . ." She burst out crying.

"Concepcion, my child," I said, distracted, "calm yourself; I love you. I will do whatever you wish."

"No," she cried, still sobbing, "no, I don't accept it! It is unheard of! I will not let you soil your name through mine. You see, now, it is I who refuse your generosity. Mateo, we will not be married before the world, but you will treat me as your wife and swear to me to protect me always. I do not ask a great thing of you; only a small house somewhere near you. And a dot. The same as you would give to the woman you would marry. In exchange, I have nothing to give you, my soul. Nothing but my eternal love, with my virginity which I have kept, through everything, for you."

XII

The climax occurs behind a barred grill.

She spoke to me in a new voice, simple and full of emotion. I felt that I had finally released her soul from the cold prison of ironic pride in which it had hidden for so long; and that a new life opened up for my moral rejuvenation.

(Have you seen in the Madrid Museum a strange canvas by Goya, the first to the left when one enters the hall on the top floor? Four women in Spanish dress, on a garden lawn, hold a shawl by its four ends, bouncing in it, laughing, a puppet as large as a man. . . .)

To be brief, we returned to Seville.

Concha had resumed her peculiar smile and her bantering tone; but I felt no more apprehension. There is a Spanish proverb which says: "Women, like cats, belong to those who take care of them." I was happy in the simple fact that she permitted me to take care of her; and I would take such good care of her!

I had allowed myself to become convinced that her pursuit of me had never faltered; that it was really she who had taken the initiative and won me little by little; that her two desertions had been justified, not by the sordid calculations I had suspected, but through my fault, mine alone, and forgetfulness of my promises. I even excused her for her indecent dance by the argument that she had despaired of ever living her dream with me, and that a virgin girl in Cadiz could not earn her bread without at least giving the impression of being a votary of pleasure. Finally, what else is there to say? I loved her.

I lost no time, but chose for her, on the very day of our r e t u r n, a *palacio*[1] in the Calle Lucena, in front of the parish of San-Isidoro. This silent quarter, almost deserted in summer, is nevertheless fresh and full of shade. I joyed in her h a p p i n e s s in this mauve and yellow street, not far from the Calle del Candelejo, where your Carmen received Don José.

The house had to be furnished. I was in haste to have it made ready, but she had a thousand caprices. A m o n g furnishers and shopkeepers we passed eight interminable days. Yet it was strangely happy, like a wedding week. Concha became almost tender, and, if she still resisted, it seemed to me that it was done gently, as though not to hurt me while keeping the promises she had made herself. I was not abrupt with her.

When I communed with myself concerning the advance of a dot to her as a mistress-wife, I recalled her reserve when she had asked this pledge of future constancy. She had not named

---

[1]Private villa.

any certain amount. Afraid of responding in-
adequately to her discretion, I turned over to
her a hundred thousand *duros,* which she accepted as though it had been a mere *peseta.*

As the end of the week drew near, I was afire
with impatience. Never did a fiancé wish more
ardently for the wedding day. I no longer
dreaded a relapse into her past coquetry, for
she belonged to me, and I felt that I understood her. I had responded to her innocent
desire for a happy life without deception. I
looked forward to long, quiet years during
which she would express freely the love which
she had not been able to hide from me on her
last night as a dancer; and I trembled with
eagerness for the joy that awaited me in the
white nuptial mansion of the Calle Lucena.

You shall soon learn how this joy was revealed to me.

The last of her whims, which I found charming, took the form of a desire to be the first
to enter her new house, which was now ready
for us both; and to receive me as a secret guest,
all alone at midnight.

Sharp on the appointed time, I arrived; the
grill was closed by bars.

I rang. After a few minutes, Concha appeared, and smiled. She wore a pink skirt, a
little cream-coloured shawl; and in her hair
were two large red flowers. I could see every
one of her features, in the strong clear light
of the moon. She approached the grill, still

smiling, and without haste.

"Kiss my hands," she said.

But the grill remained closed.

"Now kiss the hem of my skirt and the tip of my foot in its slipper."

Her voice sounded radiant.

Then she said:

"That is well. Now you may go."

My temples broke out in a cold sweat. I had a sudden dreadful premonition of all she was going to say and do.

"Conchita, my girl. . . You are laughing. . . . Tell me that you are laughing, dear."

"Oh, yes, I am laughing. I will tell you that, if it is all you want. I am laughing, I am laughing! Are you satisfied? I am laughing with all my heart! Listen, how gladly I laugh! Ha! Ha! Ha! I laugh as no one has laughed since laughter came to human lips! I am shaking, I am convulsed, I am bursting with laughter. Never have I felt so gay. I laugh as though I were drunk. Look at me closely, Mateo, to see how happy I am!"

She lifted both arms and snapped her fingers in a dancing gesture.

"Free! I am free of you! Free for all my life! Mistress of my body and of my soul! Oh, do not try to enter; the grill is too solid! But wait, you may remain a little longer. I shall not be entirely satisfied unless I show you all that is in my heart."

She came nearer and spoke close to me, her

head between her nails, in a ferocious tone:

"Mateo, I hate you. There are no words for me to tell you the horror I have of you. Were you covered by ulcers, ordure and vermin, you could not disgust me more with the touch of your skin. If God wills it, it is ended now. For fourteen months I have fled from you, and always you found me, always your hands touch me, your arms clutch me, your mouth seeks me. In the night I spat beside the bed after each of your kisses. You will never know what I endured in my flesh when you entered my bed! Oh, how much I have detested you! How I have prayed God against you! Last winter, I took holy communion seven times to have you die the day after I had ruined you. May this be as God wills it! I care no longer, I am free! Go away, Mateo, I am satisfied."

I stood there rigid as marble.

She cried again:

"Go away! Haven't you understood?"

But I could neither speak nor move; my tongue was dry, my legs frozen. She threw herself towards the staircase, and a sort of fury flamed in her eyes.

"You will not go?" she shouted. "You will not go! Very well! You will see!"

And she called in a triumphant voice:

"Morenito!"

My two arms trembled so that I shook the bars of the grill around which I had clasped my fingers.

My dazed eyes saw him descend the stairs.

She threw back her shawl and opened her two naked arms to him.

"This is he, my lover! See how pretty he is! And how young, Mateo! Look well at him whom I adore! . . . My little heart. Give me your mouth. . . Again. . . And again. . . Longer. . . How sweet my life is! . . How amorous I feel. . ."

And many other things she said to him. . .

Finally, as though she wished to extend my torture to the furthermost limits, she. . . I hardly know how to phrase it, senor. . . she united herself to him . . . there . . . under my eyes. . . at my feet.

I have still in my ears, like the remembrance of delirium, the rattle of pleasure which made her mouth tremble while mine stiffened, and the tone of her voice, when she tossed over her shoulder this parting taunt, while ascending the stairs with her love:

"The guitar is mine; I play with whom I please."

XIII

*Wherein Mateo received a visit and how
he acted upon it.*

Though I did not kill myself upon my return home, it was not because my mangled
life held out any hope for the future, but
rather because a slow anger that had finally
grown to its full strength, sustained and coun-
selled me.

Sleep was an impossibility, and I did not
even go through the formality of retiring.
Sunrise found me still dressed and pacing from
the door to the window of this room we now
occupy. I passed a mirror, and I noticed, without astonishment, that my hair had turned
grey, as you now see it.

In the morning, I was sitting at some kind
of breakfast at a table that was laid for me in
the garden. I had been sitting there about ten
minutes, without hunger, without suffering or
reflecting, when I saw, coming towards me
from the end of the alley, as though from
the depths of a dream, Concha. You need not
be surprised; I wasn't. Nothing can be foreseen, when she is in question. Each one of her
actions is always, for a certainty, stupefying
and infamous. As she walked, in her slow,
calm way, towards me, I asked myself dumbly

what infernal spirit drove her, whether it was a desire to relish still further the ruin she had wrought, or a calculation that she might, perhaps, by an adventurous maneuver, twist additional profit out of it. One or the other explanation must be the true one, I thought.

She leaned sideways to pass under a branch, closed her umbrella and her fan, and sat down facing me, her right hand resting on my table. I remember that, behind her, there was a grove, where a shining spade was planted in the earth. During the long silence which followed her arrival, a temptation obsessed me, to take that thin glittering instrument in my hand and cut her in two, there, like a small red worm. . .

"I came," she said at length, "to learn how you had died. I believed that you loved me more and that you would have killed yourself during the night."

She poured some chocolate in my empty cup and, bringing it to her mobile lips, added, as though to herself:

"Not cooked enough. It is very bad."

When she had finished, she arose, opened her umbrella, and suggested:

"Do let us go in. I have a surprise for you."

And I thought:

"I also—"

But I could not get the words out. We ascended the staircase leading to the veranda. She ran ahead, singing a well known air, slowly, to insure my understanding the application:

"And what if it should be my whim
To care not if you go with him?
You might go visiting, instead,
The bulls at Carabanchel bred!"

I followed her into a room, which she entered of her own free will. I did not thrust her in . . . what happened afterwards was not the result of any plan of mine. Our destiny was cast . . . everything had been ordered in this way. The room which she entered, (I will show it to you later), was a small one covered with rugs, silent and dark as a tomb, without any other furniture than divans. I used to go in there sometimes and smoke. It is never used now. I followed her in . . . then I locked the door without her hearing it. A wave of blood rushed to my eyes when I found myself alone with her, an anger which had been gathering, day by day, for over fourteen months. And, facing her there, I knocked her down with a blow on the face.

I had never struck a woman before. I was trembling more than she, who had fallen on her side, and who stared at me with a stupefied air, her teeth chattering:

"Mateo. . . You. . . You do that. . . to me. . ."

Then followed a torrent of violent insults, in the midst of which she cried:

"You will never strike me a second time!"

She was searching furtively in her garter, where so many women hide a small weapon, when I seized her hand and flung the knife towards a dais which reached nearly to the ceiling. Then I forced her to her knees, holding her two wrists in my left hand.

"Concha," I said, "you are not going to hear any insults or reproaches. But listen carefully: you have made me suffer beyond all human strength. You have invented moral tortures to try the soul of the only man who loved you from his heart. I now tell you that I am going to take you by force, and not once only, do you hear? But as often as it shall please me before night."

"Never! I shall never be yours!" she cried. "You fill me with horror, I tell you. I hate you like sin, like death! I hate you more than that. Kill me, then. You will never have me until you do!"

I began to beat her silently. . . I had really gone crazy; I don't quite remember all that happened . . . my eyes saw badly . . . my brain no longer thought. I remember only that I struck her again and again with the regularity of a peasant pounding a flail . . . and always on the same spots, the top of the head and the left shoulder. . . And from far off I seemed to be hearing horrible cries. . .

How long this lasted I do not know. She had not spoken a word, neither to beg for mercy, nor to abandon herself. I stopped when my fist became too painful, and then released her two hands.

She let herself fall sideways, her arms stretched before her, her head back, her hair dishevelled; then her cries abruptly changed into sobs. She wept like a little girl, always in the same tone, as long as she could without taking breath. At times it seemed as if she were going to choke. I can still see the constant twitching of her bruised shoulder, and her hands pulling the pins out from her hair. . . Then I was overwhelmed with so much pity for her and shame at my brutality that I almost forgot the shameful scene of the previous evening.

She had raised herself a little; still kneeling, her hands at her face, her eyes uplifted. . . There did not appear to be a shadow of reproach in those eyes, but . . . an almost incredible thing . . . a kind of adoration shone there. At first her lips trembled so that she could not articulate. . . Then I heard her say, in a weak voice:

"How you must love me, Mateo!"

She came nearer, still on her knees, and murmured:

"Forgive me, Mateo! Oh, forgive me! I love you also. . ."

She was sincere for the first time. But I no longer believed her. I scarcely heard her.

"How well you have beaten me, my heart!" she continued. "How sweet it was! How good it felt. . . Forgive me for all I have done to you! I was crazy. . . I did not know. . . Have

you suffered much for me?. . . Forgive me,
forgive me! Forgive me, Mateo!"

She went on in the same soft voice:

"You need not possess me by force. My
arms await you. Help me to rise. . . Did I not
tell you that I had a surprise for you? Well,
then, you shall have it presently, you shall see.
For I am still a virgin. Last night was only a
masquerade, to hurt you . . because I can say,
now, that I did not love you at all until today. But I am far too proud to take a Morenito. . . I am yours, Mateo. If God wills, I
shall be your wife this morning. Try to forgive the past, and understand my poor little
soul. I cannot explain it to you. I believe
that I am coming to life, waking up. I see
you as I have never seen you before. Come to
me, Mateo."

And, in truth, senor, she was a virgin.

XIV

Wherein it is seen that Concha's altered station does not change her nature.

That should have marked the end of our romance, and if it had, all might have been well. Alas! Why could it not have stopped there? Perhaps you shall know, one day! For misfortune never really ends in peace; a wound is never healed; never does the woman's hand which has sown anguish and tears, gather joy in the same torn field.

Eight days after that fateful morning (eight days is not a long time), Concha came in on a Sunday evening, a few minutes before dinner, and said to me:

"Whom do you think I saw? Someone I love dearly. . . Think hard. . . I am so happy."

I was silent.

"*The Morenito,*" she answered herself, gaily. "He was going through Las Sierpes, in front of the Gasquet shop. Together we went to the Cerveceria. I know that I spoke harshly of him, but I did not mean it all. He is pretty, my little friend from Cadiz. You, who have seen him, know that. His eyes sparkle under long lashes. I love long eyelashes, they deepen the gaze. And then, he has no moustache, his mouth is shapely, his teeth white. . . All the women lick their lips when they see him; he is so pretty."

"You are playing with me, Conchita. . . It is not possible. . . You have seen no one. Tell me."

"Ah, you do not believe me? As you please. . . But I shall not tell you, then, what took place later. . ."

"You will tell me at once!" I shouted, grasping her arm.

"Oh, don't lose your temper! I will tell you. Why should I not? It is my pleasure, I take it. We went together out of the city, to the Cruz del Campo. Shall I go on? We went over the whole house to pick the room with the best divan. . ."

And, as I got up, she finished, between her two protecting hands:

"And isn't it quite natural? His skin is so soft, and he is so much handsomer than you!"

What could I say? I beat her again. And ruthlessly, with an unsparing hand, partly to punish myself. She sank down in a corner, she cried, sobbed, and wrung her hands, her head bowed on her knees.

"My love, it is not true. . . I went to the bull-fight. . . I was there all day . . . my ticket is in my pocket . . . look at it. . . I was seen there by your friend G. . . and his wife. . . They spoke to me, ask them. . . I saw six bulls killed and I did not leave my seat, until it was time to leave, and I returned directly here."

[273]

"But why did you lie to me?"

"So that you would beat me, Mateo. When I sink under your strength, I love you, I love you so; you cannot imagine how happy I am when I weep because of you—come, heal me very quickly—".

And so it was to the end. When she became convinced that her false confessions no longer deceived me, and that I had every reason for believing in her fidelity, she invented new pretexts for exciting a daily anger in me. And at night, when other women say: "Will you always love me?" I heard these astounding phrases (I do not invent anything, senor): "Mateo, will you beat me again? Say that you will beat me hard! Kill me, oh, kill me! Promise me that you will kill me!"

This extraordinary predilection was not, however, the base of her character. Her perverse relish for chastisement was equalled only by her passion for sinning: not for the pleasure of doing wrong, but for the sake of inflicting pain. That was her ruling mania: sowing suffering and watching the harvest.

Jealousy, at first, was the spring of her every outrage. She quarreled so about my friends and all my acquaintances, and treated them in such an unpardonable manner, that I was soon alienated from everybody and quite alone with her. The sight of a woman, no matter of what kind or station, aroused her to fury. She turned out all my servants, from the poultry-

[274]

girl to the cook, although she knew perfectly well that I never spoke to them. In the same senseless fashion, she d r o v e away all those whom she herself engaged. I was forced to patronize different tradesmen, because the wife of one was a blonde, because the daughter of another was a brunette, and because the tobacconist asked about my h e a l t h w h e n I entered her shop. After a while I gave up play-going, because of the storms it provoked. If I looked over the orchestra seats, it was to feast on the beauty of a woman, if I turned my eyes towards the stage it was proof conclusive that I was enthralled by the actress. I even stopped walking abroad with her, for the most casual greeting became, in her eyes, an open declaration. I could neither turn over some engravings, nor read a novel, nor look at the marble Virgin, under pain of being accused of tenderness towards the model, the heroine, or the Madonna. I gave in always, I loved her so! But after what deadly ruptures!

Just as she wreaked her jealousy so savagely upon me, she maneuvered to excite mine against her, at first by fictitious devices, and then by deliberate acts. She "deceived" me, taking care to give me full details on each occasion. This original twist that she gave her intrigues left no doubt that she desired more her own excitement than mine: nevertheless, even morally, it was not a valid excuse, and, at any rate, when she returned from these flagrant adventures, I was not in a state to apologize for them, as you will readily understand.

Soon she was not content with bringing me proofs of her infidelities. She wished to re-enact the scene of the grill, substituting the reality for the sham. Yes! She actually set about surprising herself in "*flagrante delicto*" with the meticulous care that some women take to avoid it. One morning I woke up late, and missed her from my side. A letter placed conveniently at hand read as follows:

"You do not love me any more. I arose during your sleep and have gone to see my lover, Hotel X. . .' Room 6. You can kill me there if you like; the lock will be open. I shall continue my night of love until late in the morning. Come! I may have the luck to greet you during an embrace.

I adore you,
Concha."

I followed her, to what a scene you can probably imagine. Good God! There was a duel. The town shook with it. Perhaps you have heard about it. . . And to think that all this was planned "to attach me"! Up to what point can the imagination of a woman blind her toward virile love? The events of that day rose like a veil between Concha and my-self. Instead of whipping up my desire, as she had hoped, this insidious recollection spread, instead, all over her body, something odious and indelible with which she remained ever afterwards impregnated. As you could, of course, predict by now, I took her back; but my love had received its death wound. More frequent, more bitter, and more brutal quarrels followed. Through everything she clung to my life like some poisonous g r o w t h, compounded of pure egotism and selfish passion. Her fundamentally wicked soul did not even suspect that love could be otherwise. At any cost, by any means, she meant that I should remain locked in the girdle of her arms. But, finally, I escaped. It happened one day, suddenly, after one scene among a thousand, simply because it was inevitable.

A little gypsy girl, s e l l i n g baskets, had walked timidly up the garden stairs to offer her poor wares of woven rushes and reed leaves. I was about to give her an alms, when I saw Concha rush toward her and, with dire insults, tell her that she had been there the month before, that she certainly intended offering something else b e s i d e her baskets; that one could see from her bold eyes what her real profession was; that, if she went around barelegged, it was for the purpose of showing her body, and that one must be shameless indeed to go thus from door to door, with a torn skirt, seeking lovers. All this was poured out with the u t m o s t venom and in the vilest language. Then she wrenched from the poor child all her little stock, mangled it, and stamped on it. . . You can imagine the terrified sobs and writhings of the unfortunate girl. Naturally I reimbursed her for the damages, and hurried her away as best I could. Then Concha and I had our final quarrel. It was not more violent nor more tedious than the others; but it was the last. . I still do not know why.

"You would leave me for a gypsy?" she shrieked.

"No; I leave you for peace."

I arrived in Tangiers on the third day following. She joined me there. I started with a caravan for the interior, where she could not follow me, and stayed away several months during which I received no news from Spain.

When I returned to Tangiers, fourteen letters were waiting for me at the post office. I took a boat to Italy, where eight more letters reached me. Then silence.

After a year of travelling, I returned to Seville. She had been married, a fortnight before, to a young fool, otherwise well born, whom she dispatched to Bolivia with significant haste. In her last letter she had said: "I shall belong to you only, or to anyone who wants me." That she is keeping her second promise, I have little doubt.

I have told you all, my friend. Now you know the real Concepcion Perez. As for me, my life has been shattered for having met her on the road. I expect nothing from her except forgetfulness, but even that is more than I can hope for myself. This has been a painful trial of my sensibilities, but an experience so harshly acquired must and should be transmitted in such a cause. Do not wonder that I have taken the trouble to speak to you so feelingly. The Carnival died yesterday; real life begins again. For your sake, I have lifted, for an instant, the mask of an unknown woman."

"I thank you," André said gravely, shaking his two hands.

XV

*The epilogue, which prepares the reader's mind
for the moral of this story.*

It was seven o'clock in the evening when
André reached the city. He had returned on
foot. The earth lay under the impalpable enchantment of moonlight.

In order not to return the same way—or
for some other reason—he took the road to
Empalme after a long detour in the country.
The south wind permeated him with its en-
ervating warmth, which, at this hour, becomes
inexpressibly voluptuous.

As he stopped, his eyes almost closed, to
enjoy this new sensation to the full, a carriage
passed him, stopped short, and a soft voice
called to him. He stepped forward.

"I am a little late," whispered the voice,
"but you are kind to have waited for me.
Handsome stranger who attracts me, shall I
trust myself to you on this dark and deserted
road? Ah! Lord! I have no wish to die on an
evening like this!"

The look that André gave her comprehended a whole destiny. He had become very
pale when he took the empty seat at her side.
The carriage drove through an open country,
and stopped at a small green house in the

shadow of three olive trees. The horses were unharnessed and led away for the night.

. . . .

The next day, towards three o'clock, the carriage resumed its journey to Seville, and stopped at 22 Plaza del Triunfo.

André followed Concha out of the carriage, and they went in together.

"Rosalie," she said to her maid, "pack my trunks, quickly! I leave for Paris."

"Madame, a gentleman called this morning and asked to see Madame. He insisted on coming in. I did not recognize him, but he said that he had known Madame for a long time and that he would be happy if Madame would receive him."

"Did he leave a card?"

"No, madame."

Meanwhile, a servant had entered the room, and now presented Concha with a letter.

André learned a long time afterwards that it ran thus:

"My Conchita, I forgive you. I cannot live without you. It is I, now, who kneels and supplicates.

"I kiss your naked feet.

Mateo."

THE MOUNTAIN OF VENUS

I

It was in August of the year 1891, shortly
after I had heard, at Bayreuth, for the ninth
time, *Tannhauser*, *Tristan* and *Parsifal*, that
I spent a fortnight in the verdant Marienthal
near the ancient city of Essenach.

From my room I could look out upon the
lofty Wartburg, on the west, and from the
east window upon Mount Horsel, that peak
which priests and poets once called the Venusberg. And, over all, the star of Wolfram shone
in the calm clear sky of this country of
Wagner.

As I leaned my elbows upon the sill of the
western window before Luther's towers, the
spell of the Venusberg stole over me like some
magic vapour. It was that dark fascination
which had drawn me here, almost against my

[285]

will, and certainly against my native prefer-
ence, which was for sunny, placid scenes.

Unique among the neighbouring peaks, with
their garments of black firs or fertile meadows,
the Venusberg was bare of verdure and swelling like a woman's breasts. Sometimes in the
rosy dawn it was vivid with purple flesh-like
tints. At this time, and at certain hours in
the evening, it seemed to palpitate, to breathe;
and then one could imagine that Thuringia,
like a divinity reclining in a green and black
tunic, was agitated by the blood of her desires
as it mounted to the summit of her bare breast.

Every evening, like some faithful wor-
shipper, I watched this thrilling transfigura-
tion of the hill of Venus. I remained at a distance, and without desire to draw near to it.
It pleased my fancy to forget its natural existence, and revel in the exquisite joy to be
derived from simplifying realities into the pure
aspect of their symbols; to perfect this illusion,
I gazed at it from afar, where my eye would
not be affronted by actualities. I was fully
persuaded that the magic would vanish com-
pletely if once I set foot upon the mountain
itself.

Nevertheless, I was impelled at last to make
the journey. I followed, at the start, the Gotha
Road, which is intersected by bridges and
streams overgrown with foliage; then I struck
a path through the fields. I travelled for three
hours without lifting my eyes, until I reached

the end of the path. Then I looked before me.

Seen at close range, Mount Horsel was bare and reddish in aspect, having neither earth, vegetation, nor water. It appeared as if burned up by an internal fire—as if the legendary curse continued to arrest at its base all the fresh growth which clothed and g r a c e d the surrounding mountains. The path I traversed was made of stones and dead lichen, and sometimes lost itself in a stony desert, while at other times it was narrowly enclosed between high and rusty rocks. I ascended to the summit, where stood a little grey house stoutly built with thick walls to withstand the fury of the wind.

I entered the house and found that I could have lunch within. Food s e r v e d upon the Venusberg! That seemed to set the seal upon my disenchantment. Yet I welcomed the prospect, to my shame, for in spite of everything I was hungry.

The inn-keeper was absent. His two daughters spread a little table for me, upon which they placed a Wiener Schnitzl, which was perhaps more Saxon than Austrian, and a bottle of Niersteiner. There was no illusion here! The clean, light dining-room, the white curtains at the windows, the freshly-cleaned floor, the airy bedroom visible through an open door, all conspired to assure me that I was not breaking bread with witches, as for a moment, alas! I had hoped. These two young girls were good spirits, obviously, who would not assist in the damnation of the land.

True, the elder discreetly retired at the conclusion of the meal, leaving the younger, who gave me a smile of invitation which attested her natural goodness; but at German inns there are no precise limits fixed to the kindness the servants bestow upon young travellers; and that quality does not argue that they have entered into a covenant with the goddess of darkness.

We talked. She was so gracious as to understand my German readily, though I spoke it something like a negro from the Cameroons. I asked her presently for some topographical information of the country. This she was very willing to impart.

"And don't forget," she added, "to visit the grotto."

"What grotto do you mean?"

"The Venushoehle."

"Is there a grotto of Venus?"

"Oh, yes! That is its name; I don't know why. You must not go down the mountain without visiting it."

This made me uneasy, almost jealous; I wanted to know whether many strangers came to see this grotto, whose name alone sent a shudder through me.

She replied, somewhat sadly:

"Ah, no, not one! You see, the mountain is not lofty enough to tempt climbers, and for walkers, it is too high. Sometimes, at rare

[288]

intervals, a sportsman from Essenach comes to lunch or to spend the night here; but you are the first Frenchman I have seen in my life."

"What is the way to the grotto?"

"Take the path to the left. You will reach it in five minutes. Perhaps you will find a man at the entrance, seated upon a stone. But pay no attention to him, for he is mad."

So there was a grotto of Venus in the flanks of the Horselberg! But then the country of Tannhauser had retained the whole of its terrible legend.

The grotto of the Goddess was really there! And the man, too.

I soon found it. Small, elliptical at the top, and crowned with fine dark briars, it appeared as the very symbol of the mountain, still more strikingly suggestive of the old German tale than the carnal aspect of the Venusberg on the horizon. The interior, into which I gazed, was dark, narrow, and low; its dank floor composed of pools of water and mysterious recesses. The immediate certainty of becoming mud-stained tended to discourage the explorer; but some incomprehensible magnetism seemed to draw me into the humid gloom.

"Where are you going?" the man asked, shortly.

"To the bottom of the grotto."

"To the bottom of the grotto? But there is no bottom to it. It is the mouth of the earth."

"Good," I answered patiently. "I will not

[289]

get far. I shall soon return."

The other's hollow cheeks became purple. He smote his stick with his fist.

"Ah! you will soon return? Ha! ha! you imagine you can enter and depart at will! Do you think this grotto is a lift—or a geological curiosity? Are you a Cook's tourist, or do you come from a natural history museum? Is it to scratch your name upon the rock or to gather stones for your collection, that you would venture in? You are afire, perhaps, to discover subterranean lakes, blind fish, architectural stalactites and rocky arches covered with crystals! You are going to study the geology of the Venushoehle. Ha! ha! that is rich! Are you, too, a madman like the others? You, also, fail to understand. You are ignorant, then, that Venus herself is there in the flesh, with millions of her nymphs in attendance, and they are more living than you, being immortal."

"Sir," I said, "I believe you. But you much misjudge me if you think that the presence of Venus will prevent me from entering."

"Hell!" he cried.

"*That* I should not be displeased to earn, as the price of her favours."

The madman made a gesture which seemed to say: "You do not understand me at all." Then he pressed his hands upon his forehead and began to speak:

"Horselberg! or Hoelenberg, rather, the

Mountain of Hell! They come to thee without being warned of thy eternal horrors, thou who waitest for the pure, punishest the chaste, and will consume in eternity the wicked misers of the flesh. Their lonely lives they will have lived in violation of the divine law, and they will not know thy atrocious burning till the day when, by the power of the Sword, the Harbinger of Souls will plunge them into the abyss. They have eyes and they see not, ears have they and they hear not, they have mouths and they do not. . . My God, they are mad! mad! mad!"

Suddenly turning upon me he shouted:

"How can you say that the Venusberg can become a place of damnation when it is hell itself!"

I made a movement.

"Alas!" he groaned, as his hands fell from his eyes to his beard, "Alas! shall I be the only living soul to know the truth, the truth, the truth? Will it be all in vain that the patriarchs have placed Venus as the terrible antithesis of God, and will no one understand that she is Satan? Is it to no purpose that ancient tradition has depicted the satyrs with horns, black tail, goat's legs, and cloven hoofs: will no one recognize them as demons? And the flames of hell—will no one in the world understand that they are thousands of naked women dancing . ." (he struck the earth) "there beneath our feet!"

He shuddered. I stared at him fixedly.

"Ever since man has thought, written, and learned, he has repeated and cried out, in all the works of his hand, that no worse torture than love exists. How is it he has not foreseen that in the world of eternal torture that punishment alone will be inflicted upon him! What other could he imagine more terrible?"

He assumed a position as if he were gazing into the distance, and waved his hand.

"Yes," he continued, "it is there . . . it is there. . . On the day when we shall be nothing but rotting corpses and souls maddened by terror, there we shall go in crowds, the multitude of us, all sinners, to burn forever in the horrible fire which is Lust. Always, every day, every hour, we shall suffer desire at its keenest agony for more and more beautiful women, and at the moment of possession we shall see them, as on earth, disappear in smoke. But that which is here a spasm, a fear, a cry, a sob, that which suffices to prepare the curse of a human life, will be there a perpetual tremor, unassuaged anguish, and the deadly punishment of years, of centuries, and of aeons. Ah, God! such is the destiny which awaits me."

His eyes became fixed upon a stone on the ground. He went on in an altered tone, nodding his head as he spoke:

"My life has been an evil one, sir; this is the reason. I was born of Protestant parents in the Mountain of Wartburg, that same one where Luther, more than three centuries ago, taught his evil doctrine. I spent my youth in piety, and led a noble, austere life. But from my fourteenth year I could not look at a woman without experiencing frantic temptation. I curbed myself by fierce struggles which left me in the morning with a forehead bathed in sweat and twitching muscles. I thought to remain pure by living without love, mad that I was, and blind to nature itself. So eager was I to remain pure that I would have killed myself with my own hand before committing any sin. Those who have not been torn with nightly combats between religious duty and carnal desire have not tasted sorrow. I struggled thus for an illusion, and I know now that my struggle was against God. And later I got married, sir, but married only in the eyes of the world. The woman and I had sworn to unite only our souls. That was how, little by little, I was damned for my fault of lying every day to the law of life; and afterwards there was not time for me to follow the path I had missed in my youth. Ah! cursed be virgins! for the love they have crushed during their damned existence will rise to accuse them in their future state."

He seized me by the arm.

"Hark! The sun is sinking. The time approaches. Every evening I come here, and sweetly the Goddess sings. She calls me from afar; she attracts me. I come just as I did at the day of my death—yes!—at the day of my fall into the Venushoehle. Ah! do not say a word. She is about to speak to us."

I know not whether it was these last few words, the man's expression, or the clutch of his hand which persuaded me that his prediction was true; but tremors ran through me, and I listened.

I expected, not as a possibility, but with the absolute exactness of prevision, the event for which he prepared me.

My state of mind is comparable only to that of a traveller who, after seeing the lightning, and knowing how far the storm is, waits for the answering thunder.

The time which s e p a r a t e d me from the prodigy decreased first by a quarter, then a half, then three-quarters, and at the precise moment which I had anticipated as the end of my w a i t i n g, *a breath of perfumes, wafted through the cave, carried up to us the languishing echo of a . . . Voice!*

THE END

www.ingramcontent.com/pod-product-compliance
Lightning Source LLC
Chambersburg PA
CBHW011653010726
47499CB00010B/3248